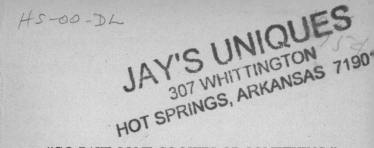
"GO BAKE SOME COOKIES OR SOMETHING," O'HARA SAID.

Already a _____  _____ lly bristled. O'Hara h_____ o work. No. His whole _____ tions of machismo. _____ e a defiant notch.

"Fine. This evening, when I get home from work, I will bake chocolate chip cookies. Then I will invite the neighbors in and serve them _café cubano_ and these freshly baked cookies. If one of them confesses, I won't hear it. Will that make you happy?"

He ran his fingers through already unruly black hair. "No, Mrs. DeWitt, that will irritate the hell out of me."

She smiled. "Perfect. Oh, and you may call me Molly."

"I'm not going to call you at all." He was gritting his teeth.

"We'll see."

A MOLLY DEWITT ROMANTIC MYSTERY

HOT

PROPERTY

SHERRYL WOODS

A DELL BOOK

Published by
Dell Publishing
a division of
Bantam Doubleday Dell Publishing Group, Inc.
666 Fifth Avenue
New York, New York 10103

The trademark Dell® is registered in the
U.S. Patent and Trademark Office.

ISBN: 0-440-21003-8

Printed in the United States of America

Published simultaneously in Canada

April 1992

10 9 8 7 6 5 4 3 2 1

OPM

HOT

PROPERTY

CHAPTER
ONE

Discovering a corpse first thing in the morning shot the hell out of Molly DeWitt's plans for getting to the office early. Outside the condominium's wall-to-wall sliding glass doors, wispy clouds scudded across a near-perfect spring sky. Faced with death, Molly had the irrational feeling that those clouds should have had the decency to shade the sun. Instead the unrelenting light streamed into the Ocean Manor cardroom, illuminating the murdered man in a macabre spotlight. She stood frozen in the doorway, her gaze fastened on the glistening serrated knife sticking out of Allan Winecroft's back. The bloodstain surrounding it had absolutely ruined his designer polo shirt, which had once been the golden color of melted butter. It now looked as if it had been tie-dyed.

Swallowing hard and staring at the mess, Molly thought about all those new condominium rules legislating absolute tidiness in all of the public areas. Allan

Winecroft had drafted every one of them. Little had he known that he was about to become the rules' worst offender. The irony of that didn't escape her. In fact, that little glimmer of gallows humor was about the only thing keeping her from screaming her head off, not so much in fear as in frustration. She was really getting tired of murders, especially in her own backyard.

Less than six months earlier Molly had sold her lovely Spanish-style house in an older bayside section of Miami because of the burglaries and because a Colombian drug dealer had been shot to death under the corner streetlamp just outside her door. She'd been watching the news at the time.

It had been a fairly routine news night, actually. There had been another home invasion robbery in Fort Lauderdale and another record haul of cocaine discovered on a decrepit fishing boat in the Miami River. More AIDS-infected needles had been found near a school playground. The sound of shots had sent Molly diving for the floor. When her knees hit the tile, she'd spent about ten seconds cursing at the pain, then reached for the phone and called a real estate agent. She'd figured someone else could summon the police.

The minute a deal for the house had been struck she'd begun looking for someplace safe for herself and her eight-year-old son. The thought of leaving South Florida had never once occurred to her, only getting away from that jinxed house where even her marriage at the end had been almost criminal in its polite emptiness. Beyond that, though, she loved

Miami's ethnic diversity, its vibrancy, even its conflicts. There was a passionate undercurrent here that either invaded the soul or robbed you blind. She wanted the passion, but was determined to minimize the danger. How many stereos and VCRs could she be expected to replace in one lifetime anyway?

In practically no time at all, she had chosen Key Biscayne. Not only was the island beautiful, but more important it was a relatively safe haven compared to Miami. Bumper stickers, faded navy blue with yellow lettering, proclaimed it PARADISE FOUND. Like all bumper sticker philosophy, the phrase held more than a grain of truth.

Only a fifteen-minute drive from downtown Miami, Key Biscayne was a world apart in attitude. The old-timers on the island, in fact, were still bemoaning the loss of the drawbridge. That bridge had intimidated most criminals. They had stayed away for fear of being caught on the wrong side with police on their heels and a yawning emptiness over Biscayne Bay ahead of them. Now an almost blinding white span climbed into the sky and curved down again, providing three lanes of clear sailing back to the mainland. The new bridge had provided easier access for developers, beachgoers, and criminals alike.

It also made Key Biscayne convenient to Molly's job. The Miami/Dade Film Commission office, which had inexplicably been made part of the parks department, was housed in the old gatehouse of the famed Vizcaya estate, practically at the end of the Rickenbacker Causeway. She could be there in exactly twelve minutes, ten if she ignored the forty-five-mile-an-hour speed limit the way everyone else did.

Having decided on Key Biscayne, Molly chose Ocean Manor partly because of its view of the Atlantic and mostly because it had beepers and Medco security keys for every entrance, plus guards at the gate, guards at the door, and a security chief who was a former Nicaraguan freedom fighter with a nasty, intimidating scar on his cheek.

Too bad one of those guards hadn't been on duty in the cardroom last night.

Although Molly was tempted to sneak right back into the elevator and pretend she'd never left her apartment, her conscience wouldn't let her. Perhaps it had something to do with the fact that the murder weapon happened to have come from her own kitchen. She recalled the last time she'd seen the knife. Drucilla Winecroft, the dead man's wife, had been using it to slice the frosted double fudge cake served following last night's heated bridge competition. The couple had lost.

Molly felt it was probably important to point out that the Winecrofts were avid bridge players. She wasn't. In fact, she was barely adequate, with bidding skills more suited to an auction than a bridge table. She had agreed at the last minute to substitute for an ailing neighbor. Within minutes she had vowed never again to be trapped into playing opposite the competitive pair. Their constant bickering over strategy throughout the evening had set her nerves on edge. If the game had gone on much longer, Molly might have been tempted to kill both of them herself. Even so, it was impossible to imagine that Drucilla had been so irate after the defeat that she'd stabbed her husband in retribution for the crummy bid he'd made in the final hand.

Attuned to the crackling tension between the couple, Molly had been very careful not to gloat as she'd laid her winning trump card—a paltry deuce—on the table. She hadn't stuck around for the debate over who the real dummy had been or for her serving of cake.

Perhaps she should have stayed, she thought as she stared at the dead man. Perhaps if she'd lingered long enough, the murder weapon would have been washed and dried and back in her kitchen where it belonged instead of stuck between the shoulder blades of the controversial president of the Ocean Manor condominium association. She didn't envy the person who had to come up with a list of suspects. Allan was hated equally by everyone except the tight coalition of residents who'd maneuvered him into office. Some suggested the election had been about as valid and free of ballot-box stuffing as those held in many reluctantly democratic Third World countries.

Without moving an inch farther into the room, Molly glanced around. There was no sign of a struggle. Not so much as a rattan chair or a chintz-covered cushion was out of place at any of the half-dozen card tables. Someone had wiped off the Formica-topped bar, clearing away the remnants of the bridge game refreshments. Even the trash can had been emptied of paper plates and cups. She had to assume the players had done all that before leaving the previous night, probably at Allan's insistence. If it had been left to the cleaning staff, and they had been in this morning to tidy up, surely they would have mentioned the body.

The manager was a stickler for discretion, but even he would expect them to acknowledge a dead man. Besides, there were a few cashews ground into the pale-peach carpet, which meant no one had been in to vacuum.

Molly wished she'd paid more attention to those college lessons in deductive reasoning. Since he was still wearing the same clothes he'd had on the previous night, the only conclusion she could reach was that Allan Winecroft had been killed after the games ended and all the card players except the killer had gone back to their own apartments. Unless they'd all stood around and watched, which she doubted. Most of them liked to be in bed by midnight, so they could make their eight A.M. tennis games or tee times. In fact, someone was probably pacing the marble-floored lobby in pricey sneakers right this minute waiting for Allan to show up.

Molly knew enough about crime scenes and murder investigations—mostly from TV and film scripts—to guess that this was going to be a very long morning. Steadying herself, she walked to the security desk in the lobby and announced . . . nothing. She couldn't seem to squeak out so much as a single word. *Dead* or *murder* would have been sufficient, but she had to settle for pointing down the hall. Apparently she looked convincingly desperate. Security Chief Nestor Perez hefted his dark-green pants over his pot belly and ambled off in the right direction. Within minutes she heard the excited babble of Spanish over his walkie-talkie. Guards suddenly appeared from every which way, running now. Lord knew who was left to open the gate for the police, who she devoutly hoped would be arriving at any minute.

When Nestor returned, he spewed what sounded like a barrage of questions at her. Molly stared at him blankly. It wasn't that she was still speechless. It was simply that her understanding of Spanish failed her when the words came at her too fast.

"*Despacio, por favor,*" she pleaded, sinking onto the bright chintz cushions of the lobby sofa. "Slowly."

"*Sí, sí,*" he promised, his head bobbing. "*¿Qué pasa?*" He gestured wildly toward the cardroom.

Molly shook her head. "I have no idea what happened. When I left last night, everyone was eating cake. My cake, as a matter of fact. It was double fudge, from some Junior League cookbook my mother gave me as a wedding present. I baked it after work. I promised Brian a slice to take to school, but I forgot to take the leftovers upstairs. I ran down this morning to get them to put in his lunch box, but it was too late. I guess it was too late. Actually I forgot all about looking for the cake, once I saw the body. Allan is dead, isn't he?"

Nestor's expression grew increasingly puzzled as she babbled on and on, uncharacteristically unable to form a simple declarative sentence.

"*¿Qué?*" he said finally. The scar on his face was drawn tight.

Molly sighed and shortened her response. "I don't know what happened."

He patted her hand, the gesture awkward but sympathetic. The scar curved with his smile like an elongated dimple. "Is okay, Mrs. DeWitt. Police come soon."

He sounded almost as relieved by the prospect as she was. "God, I hope so," she said fervently.

Nestor left her to her prayers and headed back to the action down the hall.

"Hey, Mom! Are you down here?"

Molly recognized her son's voice and jumped up, racing toward the cardroom. The thought of Brian stumbling across Allan Winecroft's body panicked her. He'd probably be traumatized for life. She'd spent days thanking God that he'd been with his father the night of the murder outside their former home. She drew in a deep breath now, preparing herself to deal with his shock. He saw her coming and ran to meet her. He skidded to a halt on the marble floor, a freckle-faced kid with a gap-toothed smile and blue eyes sparkling with excitement. He looked anything but traumatized.

"Hey, Mom, did you know there's a dead man in the cardroom? Who is it? Can I see? Juan and Nestor said I had to ask you. So can I? I never saw a dead guy before."

Molly winced. When had her child become so bloodthirsty? Was it cartoons or the evening news that had done it? Or maybe Nestor's endless reminiscences about the violence of the revolution back home? He was particularly proud of a couple of bloody ambushes he'd led.

"No, you may not see," she said firmly.

Brian obviously took the denial as nothing more than a minor setback. "What happened? Did he have a heart attack? There are a lot of old guys around here. I'll bet that's it. He had a heart attack, right?"

"No." Molly wondered exactly what the psychology textbooks had to say about explaining murdered neighbors to an eight-year-old. The textbooks probably couldn't help with a kid like Brian. He was precocious and wise beyond his years, his IQ in a range that intimidated the daylights out of her. Witness the fact that at the moment he was far more curious than scared. Maybe you had to be thirty to be shaken. Not that she was that old, but she'd been trying the age on for size ever since her twenty-ninth birthday. It still didn't fit. Fortunately, she had another four months to get used to it. God, she was still rambling.

"Why don't you meet Kevin and walk to school this morning," she suggested. When textbook answers eluded her, she'd grown into the habit of relying on evasive tactics. "I'm probably going to be tied up here awhile."

"Heck, no," Brian said. He peered at her intently. "You don't look so good, Mom. You aren't gonna be sick, are you? Was it really gross in there?"

"Gross enough," she muttered under her breath.

Brian followed her back to the sofa. He sat next to her and slid his hand into hers. "It's going to be okay, Mom."

She hugged him. "Yes, it is. Now, please, won't you go on to school?" As soon as the words were out of her mouth, she knew she should have made them sound more like an order. The truth of the matter was she didn't want him to go. Brian kept her grounded in reality. There was a lot to be thankful for in her life, but this feisty, independent kid of hers was at the top of the list.

He shook his head. "You can take me later. I'll write a note and you can sign it."

Molly glanced at him ruefully. How had she managed to raise a child who thought he was the parent? "Thank you."

Suddenly his expression grew worried. "Mom, we're not going to have to move again, are we?"

Since she had no idea where they would go next if all these guards couldn't protect them from murder, she shook her head. "No. We're not moving."

A relieved smile spread across his face. "Good. I finally figured out how to ace the tests in this school. I'd hate to have to start all over with some other teacher."

Just then two green-and-white Metro–Dade police cars roared into the circular driveway, followed by the bright yellow Fire–Rescue ambulance. At the sound of all the sirens, Nestor rushed back.

Practically delirious with self-importance, he led the police and the paramedics through the fancy lobby toward the crime scene at a clip that had him puffing before they hit the turn in the corridor. Molly briefly considered following them but decided they'd find her when they needed her. She had no particular desire to take one last look at Allan Winecroft's body, much less to get into a sparring match with Brian over why he couldn't go with her.

As she waited, two couples left for the tennis courts and one man, briefcase in hand, left for the office. All of them smiled politely. None of them bothered to question the presence of all the police. It had been Molly's observation since moving in that apartment dwellers tended to avoid overtly poking their noses into their neighbors' business. Condo and island politics gave them more than enough to gossip about over breakfast at the packed Doughnut Gallery counter.

Thirty minutes later, a muddy Jeep van turned in to the crowded drive. After an instant's hesitation while he considered the limited options, the driver wedged the oversize vehicle into the too small space between the last police car and the garage entrance. The next person hoping to get into the garage was going to have a conniption. Either the Jeep's driver didn't know Miami driving conditions or he had a death wish. Maybe he just had good car insurance.

The man who emerged was drop-dead-gorgeous, an unfortunate turn of phrase this morning, she realized, but accurate. Molly considered warning him about the parking risk he'd taken, just to save his handsome neck. He had dark hair, dark eyes, a dark suit, and a dark expression. Actually she wasn't all that sure about the eyes. They were hidden behind a pair of silvery sunglasses that reflected everything but the wearer's emotions. Molly pegged him as a cop.

After a muffled conversation with the nervous guard Nestor had posted at the door, he headed straight for the cardroom.

Thirty minutes later he was back again. This time he came straight toward Molly. His tie wasn't quite as neat as it had been, but beyond that he was as unruffled and businesslike as a banker about to conduct an interview for a loan. He'd removed the sunglasses, but he held them as if he couldn't wait to shove them back into place.

"You're Mrs. DeWitt?"

"Yes."

"Michael O'Hara. I'm with the Metro homicide division. I'd like to ask you a few questions."

"O'Hara?" She tested the Irish name and tried to reconcile it with the distinctly Latin appearance and faint Spanish accent. She couldn't.

"It's a long story," he said, apparently guessing her confusion.

Since Molly really wanted something to take her mind off Allan Winecroft's murder, she considered asking him to indulge her by telling the story now. In detail. She decided against it.

"Brian, why don't you go get your things ready for school," she said instead. "We'll leave as soon as I'm finished here."

"But, Mom . . ."

"Go. Be back in fifteen minutes and bring my purse."

"Couldn't I just ask one question?" he pleaded.

"One," she agreed.

He cast a suspicious look at the policeman. To the detective's credit, he withstood the scrutiny patiently. "If you're really a cop," Brian said, "where's your gun?"

It was an apt question, since Michael O'Hara's attire was considerably more stylish than the beige-and-brown Metro–Dade uniforms. If he had his gun in the standard blank patent leather holster, it certainly wasn't visible underneath the tailored jacket of his black pin-striped suit. This man was dressed for dinner at Les Violins and, except for the slightly askew tie, far too fastidious to be packing the bulge of an automatic weapon.

Detective O'Hara's smile was every bit as devastating as Molly had anticipated. "Don't worry, son. I can get to it, when I need it. Want to check my badge, instead?"

"Heck, no. Timmy Rogers brought his dad's to school once. It was no big deal. But I've never seen a gun up close before."

Molly nearly groaned aloud. She wondered if she ought to consult a shrink about this fascination with guns and dead men. Definitely, she decided, but later. Right now, she just wanted to get this interrogation over with and get to work where she could deal with men who just wanted locations for fictional TV murders.

"Enough, Brian. I said one question. You've asked it. Now move it."

He cast one last, longing look at the detective, but Molly's stern tone discouraged argument . . . for a change. "Yeah, okay," he grumbled and left, feet dragging in protest.

When Brian had gone, Detective O'Hara claimed the seat he'd vacated next to her. She couldn't help noticing that the man had great thighs, the thick, muscled kind ballplayers got from hunkering down behind home plate. The observation startled her, not because he did, but because she'd noticed. She hadn't had much time or inclination to think about sex lately, but suddenly it was almost impossible to think about anything else, even the murder.

Why was it that some men could turn up the female thermostat just by walking into a room? Worse, why did it always seem to happen under impossible circumstances? This man was here to investigate a murder, for God's sakes. *His* mind certainly wasn't on sex. She glanced just to be sure. He was scrutinizing his notes, not her thighs. Just as she'd thought, businesslike.

"So," he said. "Tell me what happened." His tone was as casual as a first date's inquiring about a movie plot. His eyes missed nothing. Humorless, relentless, those eyes made her very nervous. She was accustomed to flirting glances, even cool dismissals, but not this cold assessment. She almost wished he'd put those sunglasses of his back on.

"What happened when?" she asked, rattled by the distrust she sensed. She was used to being viewed as one of the good guys, an upstanding citizen.

"You choose."

If she hadn't been the target, Molly would have congratulated him on his interrogation technique. He'd left her all sorts of room to hang herself. Since she wasn't guilty, she took a deep breath, started with the bridge game, and brought him up to date. "And that's all I know," she concluded ten minutes later. Apparently he didn't think so. He still had questions.

"Was he still fighting with his wife when you left?"

"Yes."

"About the bridge game?"

"Yes," she said slowly.

He was all over the hesitation. "What else?"

"Well, if he weren't in there on the floor with a knife in his back, I might never have thought of this, but in retrospect it seems as if their argument wasn't really about bridge at all. I mean the words were, but . . ."

He pinned her with skeptical brown eyes. "Is this one of those women's intuition things or something concrete?"

"Don't dismiss women's intuition. I read a script just the other night . . ."

"A script? You're an actress?"

"You don't have to say it as if it's only one step up from working the streets," she retorted. "No. I am not an actress. I work for the Film Commission. We read scripts in advance sometimes so we can help the production company find locations. Anyway, in this script if the stupid policeman had paid attention to the star witness's intuition . . ." She caught the expression on his face. "No offense."

"None taken," he said, though it didn't sound as if he meant it.

"Anyway, do you want to hear this or not?"

"By all means, guess away."

She ignored the patronizing tone, though it was dimming his attractiveness considerably. "I can't say what it was. It was just this undercurrent. If you're married, you must know what I mean."

"Divorced," he said tersely, but his tone was suddenly less skeptical. "I think I see. Keep going."

"Okay. Nobody gets that upset about bridge unless they've been fighting about something more serious, something they don't dare fight about in public."

"But you have no idea what this other argument might have been about?"

"No. I could ask around, though. Some of the

other bridge players probably know them better than I do."

He was shaking his head before she finished the offer. "Let me ask the questions, okay? This is a murder investigation, not some TV script. You stay out of it," he ordered Molly in the tone of a man instructing the little woman to remain dutifully in the kitchen. It was his first serious mistake. Molly did not take kindly to orders, even those intended to be in her own best interests. It was a knee-jerk reaction, she supposed. It wasn't as if the man were challenging her civil rights, after all. Even so, she responded to the arrogance with her finest sarcasm. She figured he'd get the idea that she wasn't pleased.

"Much to my regret I found the body," she reminded him. "To my further regret the murder weapon matches the set of knives in my kitchen. I'd say I'm already in the middle of it."

"You said you left early last night and that the knife was still there. You dutifully called the police when you found the body and waited around to be questioned. Unless you have some motive you haven't mentioned, you're probably not a prime suspect. Unless you have a license, you're not an investigator. That puts you in a league with Nancy Drew. I don't need amateurs meddling with this case. Forget you ever stumbled on the body this morning."

"A fat lot of good that'll do you when I have to testify in court." She didn't bother to mention that she wasn't in the habit of discovering dead men first thing in the morning and that, therefore, she couldn't be quite as cavalier about it as he seemed to be. She was likely to recall Allan Winecroft's untimely demise for some time to come. She would not be able to forget it until the killer had been revealed and safely stashed behind bars.

"Back-burner it, then," Detective O'Hara advised. "Go bake some cookies or something."

Already at the end of her patience, Molly bristled. He hadn't suggested that she go on to work. No. Just *go bake cookies.* His whole demeanor screamed of generations of machismo. Hal DeWitt at his worst before the divorce couldn't have matched the implied put-down. Molly's chin automatically rose a defiant notch.

"Fine. This evening, when I get home from work, I will bake chocolate chip cookies. Then I will invite the neighbors in and serve them *café cubano* and these freshly baked cookies. If the name Allan Winecroft happens to creep into the conversation, I will ignore it. If one of them confesses, I won't hear it. Will that make you happy?"

He ran his fingers through already unruly black hair, in a gesture she'd begun to recognize about three seconds into the interrogation. "No, Mrs. DeWitt, that will irritate the hell out of me."

She smiled. "Perfect. Oh, and you may call me Molly."

"I'm not going to call you at all." He was gritting his teeth.

"We'll see."

As she stalked off, head held high, her waiting son observed, "Mom, I'm not real sure it's such a good idea to tick off a cop."

"The man investigates murders, Brian. He doesn't commit them."

"Yeah, right. You must not have seen the way he looked at you."

She had, actually. She'd been hoping it was lust. It would improve her mood considerably to see that such lust went unrequited.

CHAPTER
TWO

The more Molly thought about the marital rift theory she'd suggested to Detective O'Hara, the more she wanted to check it out herself. There had been a definitely hostile undercurrent to the tension between her bridge opponents. She'd had enough battles with her own ex-husband in public to recognize the symptoms of a volatile relationship gone sour and the wasted attempts to camouflage it. Maybe she was afflicted with the same bloodthirsty curiosity as her son, after all. She would give almost anything to be there when the police interviewed Drucilla Winecroft about her husband's murder. She considered racing the detective to the woman's apartment, but decided that would only increase his displeasure with her. Besides, what would she say to the widow?

I'm so sorry that Allan's dead. Could I get my knife back?

Or perhaps, *Drucilla, dear, did the knife slip when you were cutting the cake?*

Neither seemed quite right. Nor was she able to muster up the sincere sympathy of a close friend. She'd known the couple only casually before last night. She doubted that her winning hand had endeared her to them. En route to the car, she considered what she did know.

Though he was short and overweight, Allan Winecroft had always managed to create a distinguished impression. He dressed elegantly. Even his sports clothes looked as if they'd been ordered from a British tailor with understated taste. Only a single strand or two of gray had dared to thread its way through his impeccably styled, sun-bleached hair. Molly had heard that he'd been some sort of hotshot broker, maybe stocks, maybe land. For all she knew, it could have been frozen foods, brokered to grocery chains, that had made him rich and allowed him to retire comfortably before his sixtieth birthday. He had turned sixty-two several weeks earlier. Drucilla had thrown a lavish celebration.

As for Drucilla, she spent her days playing tennis, her evenings playing bridge, and any leftover time writing checks to local charities. Word was that Allan's money had bought her seats on several cultural organization boards since they'd taken up residence in Florida from October through April three years earlier. They spent summers on Long Island—Bridgehampton, East Hampton, one of those places where the rich summered and continued their games of tennis and bridge. In her spare time during those months, she had various body parts lifted until her skin was taut as a twenty-year-old's and her eyebrows were almost up to her carefully tended hairline. Personally, Molly found the attempts to defy age and gravity a little pathetic.

She still wanted to talk to her.

"Wait here," she told Brian, impulsiveness winning out over discretion.

"Where are you going?"

"I forgot something."

"What?"

"My briefcase."

"I could get it, while you get the car."

She glared at Brian, which he didn't deserve. "I'll do it. Here, take the keys and wait in the car. It won't take a minute." If it took any longer than that, she was likely to come face-to-face with the detective in the corridor. As attractive as he was, it was not an encounter she cared to have. She had a feeling he'd have a temper to go along with that hot-blooded Latin machismo of his.

After casting a quick glance in the direction of the cardroom to make sure that Detective O'Hara was still occupied, Molly raced to the elevator. For once it was on the lobby level. It whisked her to the eighth floor before she could fully formulate her questions for Drucilla.

The Winecrofts had bought two apartments facing the ocean and combined them into what Molly had heard described as a showcase of excess. No one had ever explained to her satisfaction what they did with two full kitchens, especially since they never seemed to eat at home. At any rate, she approached the special double doors they'd had installed and rang the chim-

ing bell, also their own touch. Most people in the condominium had settled for the brass knockers installed
by the builder ten years earlier.

Molly braced herself to deal with the weeping
widow. When a petite Salvadoran housekeeper with a
perfectly placid expression opened the door instead,
she momentarily was taken aback.

"Is Mrs. Winecroft in? I'm a neighbor, Molly De-
Witt. We played bridge together last night. I just
wanted to express my condolences."

Round brown eyes stared at her in confusion. *"Sí,"*
the woman said finally, but without apparent comprehension. She struggled for words. "She asleep." She
folded her hands together and rested her head against
them in case her meaning wasn't clear. "Asleep, *sí?*"

"Asleep," Molly repeated. "You mean she doesn't
know?"

"¿Qué?"

She didn't know, Molly surmised. Neither of them
knew, not the housekeeper and definitely not the
sleeping widow, unless she was a cold-hearted bitch.
Since Molly did not have the least desire to be the one
who broke the news, she waved politely. "I'll see her
later."

She stepped straight back into the waiting arms of
Detective O'Hara. She knew they were his because she
recognized the suit. To her disgust, she realized she
wouldn't mind lingering longer so that she could recognize his embrace. In case it happened again. Under
other circumstances, that is. It wasn't men who be-
trayed women, she decided in disgust. It was women's
own undiscriminating female hormones that lured
them into relationships with the wrong men.

"Imagine meeting you here," he said. He didn't sound overjoyed.

"She doesn't know," Molly whispered with a certain amount of urgency as the housekeeper cast shy, appreciative glances at the detective. Molly felt a little less guilty knowing that his appeal was universal.

Not the least bit sidetracked by his hormones he said, "Unless she did it and took a sedative."

Molly grimaced at the cynicism, even as she admired the astuteness behind it. "I never thought of that."

"That's why I'm a policeman and you're a whatever it is you are."

He still didn't sound especially interested in being more informed about her career. She supposed it was extraneous. However, since she was proud of it and irritated by his attitude, she told him anyway. "An administrative assistant."

"Does that pay better than secretary?"

"Are you intentionally trying to provoke me or does it just come naturally?"

"I'm trying to conduct a murder investigation."

"Then maybe you shouldn't be so quick to insult a witness."

Amusement dashed across his lips so quickly, she almost missed it. Fortunately, since she'd been considering slugging him in the teeth at the time, her gaze had been fastened on her target. "Unless I missed something earlier, you didn't actually see the murder, right?" he said.

He had her there. "Well, no," she admitted with great reluctance. She could see where this was headed. It was not going in her favor.

"Then as a witness, you're of limited value to the case. I can spare you."

"The state attorney might not see it that way."

"Then let that office deal with you."

The housekeeper's round, dark eyes were follow-ing this exchange with evident fascination. "Look," Molly said finally. "This isn't getting us anywhere. You don't want me here. My son needs to get to school. I'm off." She meant to appear gracious about it. She sounded miffed. Which she was. A savvy detective wouldn't miss it. From the amused expression back on Michael O'Hara's face, he hadn't.

Before she could take the first step, she heard Drucilla inquire sleepily, "Conchita, who's out there at this ungodly hour?"

Ungodly? Ten o'clock? Molly hadn't slept that late since college, when she'd scheduled all of her classes after noon to accommodate her need for rest after waiting tables until midnight. She delayed her depar-ture to catch a glimpse of the woman who thought their midmorning arrival so ill timed.

Pulling a bright orange silk wrapper around her, Drucilla swept into place at the housekeeper's side. Though she appeared only half awake, her makeup was flawless and not one strand of her auburn hair was mussed. Unless her hairdresser lacquered it with acrylic, she'd worked to achieve that perfection.

"Molly, what on earth?" Her gaze traveled from Michael O'Hara's polished loafers to his rumpled hair . . . approvingly. Another casualty, Molly thought. The man probably had an ego the size of Texas.

"Who are you?" Drucilla inquired.

Her eyes flared slightly when he introduced himself and flashed his badge for her inspection. "A policeman? How fascinating. Come in, won't you? *Café, por favor,* Conchita."

Molly hesitated, uncertain of her own welcome. Drucilla waved her inside. "Come, Molly. I assume you're together. Did someone steal a deck of cards last night?"

As she stepped inside, Molly cast a triumphant look at the detective. She wasn't actually thrilled at the prospect of being there when Drucilla came unglued at the news of her husband's death, but the idea of being a thorn in Michael O'Hara's side made her morning. For an instant she thought he was going to dismiss her, but instead he motioned her toward the living room, graciously, as a matter of fact. Molly took it as a deliberate comment on her own surly manners.

In the huge, sunny room, which offered sweeping views of the ocean, Molly had to control the desire to wander. She felt as if she'd stumbled into an art exhibit. Competing with the Atlantic on the east was an entire wall filled with a single modern painting in splashes of sea green, sky blue and sunset orange. It lacked subtlety. It did, however, provide the room with its color scheme, all shades of blue, green and orange designed to enhance Drucilla's own vibrant coloring. Lush plants decorated the balcony. Inside, more plants provided the backdrop to pedestals topped with sculpture. Every surface was crammed with jade carvings, twists of copper, and hammered tin. Though she couldn't identify the abstract designs, Molly suspected none were ashtrays. She stared at an ivory piece that appeared to be . . . intimate. She blushed when Michael O'Hara caught the direction of her fascinated gaze. It was the second time that morning she caught the faint twitch of stubborn lips as he fought a smile. It was the second time she considered assaulting a police officer.

He turned back to their hostess. Or his chief suspect, to be more precise. "Mrs. Winecroft, I understand you were playing bridge with Mrs. DeWitt and several others last night."

"Yes."

"What time did you leave the cardroom?"

"Shortly before midnight, I would say. Why?"

"And what did you do then?"

"I came upstairs and went to bed. Why?"

"Was your husband with you?"

"No. He stayed behind to talk business."

Molly noticed that Drucilla didn't bother to ask why. Apparently she'd finally realized this was going to be a one-sided interrogation. The parameters had been set. She'd been assigned to give the answers. The detective was the only one who got to ask questions.

"With whom was he talking?" O'Hara continued.

"I don't recall. Henry Davison, I suppose. Juan Gonzalez stopped by for coffee. He doesn't play bridge." She glanced at Molly. "Who were the other men there last night?"

"Tyler Jenkins and Roy Meeks," Molly responded, then wondered why Drucilla was being so deliberately vague about a group of people who obviously played together regularly.

"Yes, of course." Her dismissive tone indicated the two were of little importance. Since Roy Meeks had been Molly's winning partner, she could understand the reluctance to acknowledge him. As for the others, her forgetfulness made little sense.

"And did your husband have business with those men?"

"No, I don't believe so. They were just chatting about the stock market, the new hotel here on the island, things like that. General conversation. Really, Detective, I don't understand what you're getting at here."

"Did you and your husband argue last night?"

This time Drucilla cast an anxious look at Molly. Long, smooth, ageless fingers, tipped with bright-red nails and adorned with impressive chunky diamonds, worried the sash of her dressing gown into a knot. "No more than usual. After thirty-five years of marriage, we have our ups and downs."

"Which are you having now?"

Drucilla calmly picked up her cup of coffee, but couldn't disguise the shaking of her hand. The hot liquid splashed on her silk gown, staining it in a way that reminded Molly all too vividly of the brown stain soaking Allan's shirt. Drucilla bit back an oath, waved off the detective's offer of a handkerchief, and with supreme effort gathered her composure around her as if it were a mink stole. There was barely a tinkle of china against china as cup met saucer.

"Detective, I have a luncheon to go to today. If you're finished."

"Not quite yet. What time did your husband return to the apartment?"

"I have no idea. As I said, I went to bed. Now, really, I must get ready."

"You may want to change your plans."

Drucilla stared at him in astonishment. "Why would I want to do that?"

"I'm very sorry to have to tell you this, Mrs. Winecroft, but your husband is dead."

The blurted announcement, coming during questions that under other circumstances might have been no more than polite chitchat, took even Molly by surprise. The man's timing sucked. She stared at Drucilla, expecting hysterics. When none came, she decided maybe O'Hara had accomplished exactly what he'd set out to do: get a completely honest reaction.

Drucilla appeared to have been stunned into silence. Time stood still for a heartbeat. Then confusion flickered in her green eyes. The announcement was either news or she was a better actress than the celebrity model currently starring in the television pilot being shot on Miami Beach.

"Allan? Dead? That can't be." Her voice was barely above a murmur. There was a distinct catch in it. "His heart is fine. He just had his physical. I'm sure, absolutely certain the doctor said he was okay. Where . . . ?"

She stared helplessly at Molly, as if looking for confirmation. At this hint of vulnerability, contrived or not, Molly was suddenly overcome with more compassion than she'd expected to feel. She moved to Drucilla's side and clasped her fidgeting hands. They were icy cold. There were still no tears.

Though his voice had softened, Michael O'Hara was relentless now, imparting information faster than the just-bereaved widow could accept it. "It wasn't a heart attack. Your husband was murdered, Mrs. Winecroft. He was stabbed, right here at Ocean

Manor. I really need you to help me discover who did it."

Drucilla trembled as his words hit home. Any help she was likely to offer was going to be delayed. With one quiet gasp, she proceeded to faint in Molly's arms.

"Well, that was certainly tactful," Molly said, as she patted the woman's wrists.

He shrugged off her indignation. "I've learned it's better just to get the bad news over with."

"Then why didn't you tell her the minute you walked in the door. 'Hello, your husband's dead.' That sort of thing?"

"I wanted a couple of uncensored answers first."

"Is that legal?"

"Legal enough."

Molly cast a skeptical glance at him and wondered what the Supreme Court had to say about that. She decided—wisely, probably—to keep her inexpert legal opinions to herself.

"Get Conchita. Maybe she has some smelling salts or something. Unless, of course, you have time for her to languish like this until she comes to on her own."

He started to argue, then shook his head and headed in the direction of the kitchen. Molly heard him and the housekeeper conversing in fluent Spanish. When he reappeared, he was carrying a damp cloth and smelling salts. Conchita was trailing along behind, wringing her hands and muttering what sounded like prayers in rapid-fire Spanish that eluded Molly's comprehension.

As much as she wanted to stay and see the scene played out, Molly knew if she didn't get to work in the next half hour, she was very likely to end up every bit as dead as Allan Winecroft. She didn't want to look that bad the next time Michael O'Hara saw her.

Before she could go, though, Drucilla began to come to. She blinked once, then impatiently pushed away the smelling salts.

"Damn Tyler Jenkins," she said. She said it fervently enough that there was little doubt about who she thought had murdered her husband.

CHAPTER
THREE

Michael O'Hara didn't have the smug look of a man who'd just wrapped up a murder case in less time than it usually took to get a car emission system inspected in Dade County. Molly could practically see him mentally ticking off the evidence and comparing it to his own gut instincts. She certainly was.

Tyler Jenkins had access to the murder weapon. He had the opportunity. The only thing missing was a motive powerful enough to incite a sixty-eight-year-old man who'd once marched for peace to commit a cold-blooded murder. Personally, Molly was also struggling with the concept that a man just recovering from by-pass surgery had enough strength to wield that knife in a deadly manner. The detective seemed equally skeptical without ever having met the man. Experience had apparently taught him to beware of quick, tidy solutions.

"Tell me why you think Tyler Jenkins is responsi-

ble for your husband's death," he suggested to
Drucilla.

Drucilla appeared startled. "Oh, I doubt that
Tyler killed him," she said. "The old goat wouldn't
have the gumption."

Not by so much as the flicker of an eyelash did
O'Hara indicate that he was disappointed or even surprised. Molly, however, had been hoping to have this
whole thing wrapped up before she left for work.

"What then?" he said to Drucilla.

"Tyler was responsible for getting Allan to run for
the presidency of the condominium association,"
Drucilla explained. "We haven't had a peaceful moment since that awful election. Just last week someone
called in the middle of the night and threatened Allan."

Molly was stunned. She couldn't imagine any of
her neighbors stooping to late-night threats. The residents of Ocean Manor were all relatively well-to-do,
well educated, and presumably civilized. Her own
modest income was probably pocket change to a ma-
jority of the owners. Many of them owned two resi-
dences, this one and an old family home up north or a
summer place in a resort area such as Aspen or Vail or
Newport. Many were South American or European.
Most seemed too busy perfecting their tans to indulge
in such skulduggery.

Of course, she admitted, the election had been
every bit as nasty as some hotly contested senatorial
race. Campaign diatribe had been slipped under the
doors on an almost nightly basis. And the contentious
annual meeting had proved beyond a doubt that pos-
sessing money did not always imply an understanding

of social niceties. Her good neighbors had fought like hellions over everything from wall sconces to cable TV. On second thought, perhaps Drucilla's claim wasn't so farfetched after all.

"Did he recognize the caller?" Molly asked. "Was he certain it was another resident?"

"That's what he said, but he didn't explain how he knew. He didn't want me worrying. He dismissed it as a childish prank by someone old enough to know better."

"And he didn't state the nature of the threat," Michael O'Hara said.

"No."

"Did he say whether it was specific, like a threat to slash his tires, or just a vague threat to get him in some way?"

"He didn't say, but it must have been a death threat. Isn't that obvious now?"

Molly certainly thought it was. The detective looked less convinced. The department must issue skepticism along with the badge, or maybe the fact that it was ingrained was what had made him choose to be a cop.

"Any other enemies?" he asked. "Old business rivals? Maybe he clashed with someone over a debt or gave someone bad business advice."

"I can't think of anyone. Allan was capable of irritating people. He had an abrasive personality, but I can't imagine him making anyone angry enough to drive them to murder."

The detective nodded. "If you think of anyone, you'll let me know."

"Certainly."

At the door, he paused for just an instant. "I really am very sorry, Mrs. Winecroft." There was a warmth in his eyes that hadn't been there before, a hint of genuine compassion. Molly had to revise her opinion of him all over again. He might be suspicious and cynical, but that was what he was paid for. Underneath the official act, he was not without sympathy.

He was, however, all business when he turned back to Molly. "Coming, Mrs. DeWitt?"

It sounded more like an order than a question. Because she had to get to work anyway—and only because of that—Molly dutifully followed him into the corridor. There was no point in lingering. Within the next hour there would be an endless parade of curious people along to console Drucilla. No doubt she'd want to change into more subdued attire before they arrived. Her scanty tears had barely streaked her makeup, and every coat of mascara was still right where she'd put it before greeting them, but that orange wrapper was a jarring note. Molly wondered if the killer would be among those offering condolences. The very thought made her shiver.

When the door had closed behind them, Michael stuffed his hands in his pockets and turned to Molly. "So, what'd you think?"

"You're asking me?" She was torn between shock and the heady sort of pleasure she always felt when some producer asked her opinion about his million-dollar script.

"You know her better than I do. Was it all an act?"

"If it was, it was a good one."

"Good, not perfect," he corrected. "She was supposedly asleep when you arrived, right?"

"That's what the housekeeper said."

"Then is it only the women I know who take forever putting on their makeup?"

Molly shot him a look of grudging admiration. She saw exactly what he was getting at. "You think she was actually awake and expecting company. The police?"

"I was thinking more in terms of a lover."

Once again Molly understood why he'd reached detective status and she was an amateur. Her mind wasn't nearly devious enough.

"Have you heard any rumor to that effect?" he asked.

"No, but I've lived here only a short time. With my hours at work, I try to spend most of my evenings with my son. I know only a few neighbors really well and they're mostly the year-round folks." Once again it occurred to her to invite them all over for tea and an informal chat. That was what Nero Wolfe might have done, though he usually waited until he had the evidence to pin the murder on one of his guests.

As if he'd read her mind, Michael O'Hara said, "Don't go snooping around on your own. What were you doing at Mrs. Winecroft's apartment anyway?"

"I explained that. I wanted to pay my respects."

He regarded her skeptically. "So you said. At least you're consistent. You intrigue me, though, Mrs. De-Witt. For a woman who stumbled on a body this morning, you're awfully calm."

Calm? She was quaking inside, but years of practice had taught her to hide her fears. Since he seemed to find her self-control damaging, she admitted, "It's all a facade, Detective."

His intent, curious gaze locked with hers. "Really?

It might be interesting to see what happens when that facade is stripped away.''

Molly wasn't one bit sure, as he sauntered away, if he was interested as a man or as a cop. Then she wondered if it was even possible for a man like Michael O'Hara to separate the two.

• • •

Brian had a thousand questions about why Molly had been delayed. She forestalled them by stopping at Vernon's and buying him French toast with powdered sugar sprinkled on it. It was his favorite and a rare treat. She sipped a cup of coffee while he ate. The place was still busy, but the islanders had gone, leaving the drugstore's three U-shaped counters to tourists. None of them had heard yet about the murder or Molly's connection to it, which left her with ten peaceful minutes to think about everything that had happened.

"Mom," Brian said, powdered sugar on his cheeks and milk on his upper lip, "who do you think killed Mr. Winecroft?"

She whirled around so fast, she almost spun off the stool. "Why do you think someone killed him? You didn't go back there, did you?"

Brian wiped the powdered sugar away with the back of his hand, ignoring the napkins in front of him. "Come on, Mom. With all the cops and everything, it doesn't exactly take a genius to figure it out. Why else would they come? Do you think we'll get finger-printed?"

She'd wondered about that herself. Not Brian, of course. But there was every reason to anticipate that she would be, if only to eliminate which prints were hers on the murder weapon. "I suppose I might be," she admitted.

"But not me?"

"You weren't in there."

"Maybe Detective O'Hara would let me be, if he's not still mad at you. You could ask him."

Molly sighed. "Brian, I am not going to drag you off and have you fingerprinted just to add a little excitement to your life."

"It'd be great for show-and-tell. I'd probably get an A."

"If it takes being fingerprinted to earn a top grade, you just may have to settle for a B."

"I'll never get into some fancy school with lousy grades. Isn't that what you and Dad are always telling me?"

"Your father tells you that. I just want you to do your best."

"Maybe I could talk to Detective O'Hara myself."

"You do and I'll ground you for a year with no Saturday morning cartoons or video games."

Brian's eyes were wide as saucers by the time she'd finished the threat. "You really don't like that guy, do you?"

"He's just doing his job," she said, deciding a little circumspection was called for, especially since her feelings were oddly contradictory. Her son had been known to innocently blab her opinions far and wide. The prospect of his sharing his astonishing insights with the detective did not please her. In fact, before he shared any more with her, she hurried him off to

school, a written excuse in hand. He'd drafted it himself, printing it neatly on lined notebook paper.

She should have had him jot one down for her as
well. Her boss scowled ferociously when she finally
walked in. Molly scowled right back at him. She was in
no mood for one of his snits this morning.

"You're late," Vincent Gates announced unneces-
sarily. He glanced pointedly at the clock that hung on
the wall opposite her desk in the cramped film office.
It was twenty-five after eleven.

"I can tell time, Vince. Don't start on me. I've had
an awful morning."

His management duty taken care of, he settled
into his more familiar sulking posture. He reminded
her of a pouting star, upset over an unflattering camera angle. "You've had an awful morning? If you'd
been here, you'd know the real meaning of awful. The
mayor's furious because he got caught in a traffic jam
on the Rickenbacker Causeway."

"Which mayor and how is that our fault?"

"The county mayor. He's blaming us because it
was caused by gawkers watching the filming of that
new soft drink commercial."

Molly hadn't expected sympathy from Vince. The
man had the sensitivity of a coconut shell. She had
accepted that within a week after taking the job with
the Miami/Dade Film Commission. He had one
agenda in life, his own. Unless she'd been personally
murdered in her sleep, he didn't think it should interfere with her work. It was pointless to belabor her own
lousy morning.

"The sexist ad with all the women in bikinis?" she
asked dutifully.

Vince glared at her. His own opinion of all the bouncing boobs was much more liberal. She was surprised he hadn't been out there gawking himself. Then, again, the producer had left a copy of the storyboards with him so he could indulge his fantasies at his leisure.

"That's the one," he confirmed. "I'm not sure if he was more upset about the slowdown on the causeway or because his view was blocked. On top of that Larry Milsap called. He needs the permits to shoot in Crandon Park no later than three. He's running over budget and they want him to finish up by the weekend. I can't find the damned things on your desk. I told him you'd run them over the minute you got in. I expected you hours ago," he added accusingly.

Molly lost patience. It rarely took longer than five minutes with Vince to accomplish that. "And I expected to be here hours ago. I was detained by a murder. I would have called, but they wouldn't let me near a phone. I guess it's only the accused who gets to make a phone call." Okay, so she was stretching the truth a little. Without missing a beat, she added, "I sent those permits to Larry last week. He's lost them again. I'll get him a new set."

Vince's irritated expression faltered. "Forget the permits for a minute. What's all this about a murder? Run it by me again."

The only thing Vince loved more than seducing women was gossip and intrigue. For the next minute or two, she had him right where she wanted him. "Only if you'll get me a very large cup of very strong coffee."

He didn't waste time protesting that serving coffee

was beneath him. He grabbed the mug from her desk and filled it from the pot sitting on the credenza at the back of the conference room. "Drink. Then talk. Fast. We don't have all morning."

"Your concern is touching."

"Okay. Okay. I'm concerned. That goes without saying."

"Vince, almost every kind, compassionate thought you ever have, assuming you have any, goes without saying. Some of us would occasionally prefer to hear the words spoken aloud."

He blinked. "You're upset." He seemed startled by the concept. Since flashes of such insight were rare with him, she could understand why.

"Bingo," she confirmed.

"At me?"

"Among others."

"Why?"

"Vince, I started my day by discovering that our condo president had been stabbed in the back."

"So what? I thought you said he was a pompous ass. Isn't he the one who dug up all the rare tropical plants and replaced them with impatiens?"

"Please don't share what I thought of his gardening taste. At this point, it might be considered a motive."

"They don't know who did it?"

"They don't know who. They don't know why. The only thing they seem to know for sure is that I found the body and that he was killed with one of my knives."

"Holy shit!"

"That about sums it up."

"You want to go home?"

This time it was Molly's turn to gape in astonishment. Vincent was not in the habit of doling out leave time. "No, thanks," she said, wondering if she should have taken it just to establish a precedent.

"Oh." He hesitated. "Then I guess you might as well take care of those permits."

She sighed. "Right away. By the way, if you'd get Jeannette to do the filing she was hired to do, you'd be able to find the permits yourself."

"I refuse to tangle with that woman."

Molly barely suppressed a grin. The Haitian clerk absolutely adored muttering imprecations that could be interpreted as curses. Vincent was convinced if she aimed one at him it would forever limit his prowess as a stud. He hadn't issued a direct order to Jeannette since her first week. When it suited him, he claimed it was Molly's job to run the office. It did not suit him, however, to pay her accordingly. Therefore, it frequently didn't suit her to run the office. Meanwhile the filing was stacking up.

Molly found the permits for Larry Milsap's Palm Productions and grabbed her purse. She stuck her head in Vince's office. "I'm off to see Milsap. If he calls, tell him . . ."

Guessing the snippy comment that was to come, Vince substituted his own more politically sound version. "I'll tell him we're absolutely thrilled to be of service. The man spends three hundred fifty thousand dollars a year on production in the county. Even if he wastes a small portion of our time, it's worth it."

"Then let him waste your time." She held out the permits.

"I have meetings all afternoon."

"You mean you're playing golf with some Holly-wood producer again, hoping he'll let you on his set to ogle his starlets."

"I don't ogle."

"Like hell," she muttered, turning away to grab the ringing phone. "Yes."

"Molly, what the hell's going on?" her ex-husband demanded.

Molly had to swallow a groan. The day had just gone from bad to worse. When Hal DeWitt had that tone in his voice, it meant nothing but trouble.

"Could you be more specific?" she replied cautiously.

"I just heard about the murder. It's all over the goddamned radio. I told you moving there was a mistake, but would you listen? No, you had to prove yourself. Well, I'm telling you now, I want my son out of there."

"Our son," she reminded him furiously. "Brian is *our* son, though frankly, there are times when I regret your role in that more than I can tell you."

"I'm picking him up today."

"You do and I'll slap you with a court order so fast it'll make your head spin." Her own head was pounding. There hadn't been one conversation since she and Hal divorced that he hadn't found some way to let her know how inept he thought she was, how unfit a mother. He'd threatened her with a custody battle so often, she should be used to it by now, but she wasn't. Even though she knew rationally that he didn't have a shred of evidence on his side and that the accusations were the unjustified slurs of a sick, pitiful man who thrived on demeaning her, it didn't stop her from trembling with fear.

"I have to go. We'll discuss this sometime when you can be more rational about it," she said. Her voice was calm and deliberate, but inside she quaked as she replaced the phone in its cradle.

"You okay?" Vince asked.

"Just fine," she snapped, turning away and straight into the arms of Detective O'Hara. Again. She took a deep breath before meeting his eyes.

"Running away?" he inquired.

At the moment, the idea of fleeing held tremendous appeal. "No," she said with a sigh. "Just doing my job."

"Which is?"

"At the moment it's delivering permits to an irresponsible producer."

"Mind if I tag along?"

"I thought you had a murderer to catch."

"I do. I told you I'd be in touch."

"I wasn't expecting you to show up quite this soon. I'm flattered that you're willing to take time out of your busy investigation schedule to be with me. Wasn't it just a couple of hours ago that you told me to stay far, far away from this case?"

"Something's come up. Could we do this someplace private?" he suggested, apparently catching sight of the fascinated gleam in Vince's eyes.

"Your car or mine? I have to get these permits out to Crandon Park before Vince ruptures a blood vessel."

"Before we lose thousands of dollars in revenue in

this county,'' Vince corrected, not bothering to hide his eavesdropping.

''You tell me where else Larry Milsap is likely to shoot a commercial on Miami tourist attractions,'' she snapped back. ''Never mind. Come on, Detective.''

''I had someone drop me off. You drive,'' he said. ''Maybe I'll catch you speeding.''

''Don't tell me homicide detectives give out tickets in their spare time.''

''Don't test me. Actually, I was thinking of it more as a test of your moral character.''

Molly glared at him, but led the way to her prized white convertible, one of her rare indulgences. When she'd turned onto Miami Avenue, she asked, ''Since when did my morals come into question?''

''Since I found out that the knife used to kill Mr. Winecroft is covered with just one set of fingerprints. Since you admit owning the knife and bringing it last night, I think we can assume for the moment that they're probably yours.''

There was a sudden sinking sensation in the pit of Molly's stomach. The implications were not heartening. ''Just one set? You're sure? Maybe the murderer's are blurred.''

''One set. We're going to need yours to match them up in the lab, of course.''

''But his wife used that knife to cut the cake last night.''

''No prints, unless you'd washed that knife clean and carried it downstairs wrapped in a towel. Did you?''

''Of course not. Dammit, I watched Drucilla cut that cake.''

"Did she wear gloves?"

"Look," she said impatiently, "I know society types tend to dress up for all occasions, but I can assure you that little white gloves would have been out of place at the bridge table. Someone would have noticed. Besides, how would she have handled the cards?"

"How about those clear plastic throwaway gloves used by kitchen help?"

"I didn't see any. You don't seriously think I killed him, do you?" She was not proud of the little catch in her voice. She really did not want to be a serious suspect in this case—or any other, for that matter.

"Let's just say I'm confused. I have a theory I'd like to throw out." He glanced at the speedometer as she approached the Rickenbacker toll booths. Molly automatically lifted her foot off the accelerator as she guided the car into the emblem lane that provided access for residents who paid an annual fee. Then she noted that she was going only five miles an hour anyway. He grinned. "Guilt is a fascinating emotion, don't you think?"

"I am not guilty, either of speeding or murder." She crept through the lane to make her point.

"Just listen to my theory. What if Mrs. Winecroft used the knife to cut the cake, then wiped it clean. Her prints would be gone."

"But so would mine."

"Not if you came back later and used the knife to stab her husband."

The words landed as if they'd been dropped from the top of a thirty-story high rise. Inane individually, together they packed quite a punch, the sort of punch that could send her to prison. She was still reeling as she pulled to the edge of the road and hit the brakes. She whirled on him furiously.

"That's a really crummy theory. Why the hell would I do that? I don't have a motive. I even won the damned bridge game."

"That is a problem," he admitted.

"Why couldn't she have wiped it clean and then used the knife?"

"Why would she bother to wipe off your fingerprints and leave her own?"

"Hell, I don't know. You're so great at coming up with theories, you figure it out."

"I'm working on a couple of ideas."

"How lovely. Would you care to share them with me?"

"Not yet."

She scowled at him. "We are talking about my motives here, aren't we? Don't you think I have a right to hear your speculations on the subject?"

"Sure. Later, after I've tested them on a few other people and we have those fingerprints ID'd positively as yours."

Molly glanced at the stunningly blue water on either side of the causeway and tried to grasp some of the serenity the sight always brought her. Instead, this gnawing sensation seemed to be eating a hole in the pit of her stomach. "You really know how to ruin a perfectly beautiful day, don't you?"

"Most people would have considered the day ruined the minute they found the body. Unless, of course, you were glad to see the man dead." He fixed her with a penetrating gaze that could have drawn a confession from the most professional criminal. She wasn't even amateur. It rattled the dickens out of her.

"How did you feel about Mr. Winecroft?" he asked.

Molly recalled her very recent conversation with Vince and decided Michael O'Hara would not have to use thumbscrews to get her boss to share her views. "I was not overly fond of some of his decisions," she said cautiously.

"Such as?"

"I hated the impatiens."

"The what?"

"All those little pink and white flowers."

His lips twitched. Apparently he didn't view that as a motive for murder any more than she did. "And?" he prodded.

"You don't think those crummy little flowers provide a powerful motive? They wilt in the heat. They look thoroughly bedraggled by noon."

"I'm sure that's distressing, but there must be something more."

"Okay, there are the assessments. They keep going up. I know the cost of living is going up, too, but there's been a lot of talk of mismanagement. The owners will end up paying, no matter who's at fault. That's tough for the people on fixed incomes."

"Even if they're fixed in the millionaire range?"

"Not everyone in that building is filthy rich. Just as an example, if I hadn't sold my house, in which I had a fair amount of equity, I couldn't have made enough of a down payment to whittle the mortgage down to a size I can manage."

"So if the assessments go up, your apartment's at risk?"

Oh, hell. Nice work, Molly. She had just provided herself with a motive. "I really shouldn't have said that, right?"

He grinned. "An attorney would have advised against it. However, the fact that you did suggests to me that you're not a hardened killer."

"And the person who did this is?"

"A killer has to be pretty motivated, either by anger or a long-standing and deep-seated grudge to stab someone. It's not a clean method of killing. Women generally prefer poison or even a dainty but deadly shot."

"So I'm off the hook?"

He grinned. "Not entirely. I wouldn't leave town, if I were you."

"You will let me know when you're convinced, I'm sure."

"Absolutely. Until then I think you can expect to be seeing a lot of me."

If almost any other drop-dead-gorgeous man had said that to her, she might have been thrilled. Knowing that this man considered her capable of murder more or less took the edge off her anticipation.

CHAPTER
FOUR

Molly DeWitt, onetime debutante, a murder suspect? All her life she had fought against being categorized as some frivolous airhead just because her parents had insisted on putting her through the tortures of a debutante ball. Compared to being a murder suspect, however, those days had been heavenly.

Reluctantly, she tried the suspect label on for size. It was ludicrous, but there was no denying that the evidence could be interpreted that way if another candidate didn't turn up. Even though Michael O'Hara seemed competent and she'd been taught—naïvely, perhaps—that the police were friends of the innocent, she wasn't about to take any chances. She'd better find the real murderer herself. The alternatives, including turning her son over to Hal DeWitt to raise while she went to jail, were unacceptable.

Highly motivated by the time she dropped Detective O'Hara at the Key Biscayne police station and undaunted by his repeated warnings to stay out of it, she planned her own informal investigation. She would interrogate every one of those present last night, starting this afternoon.

She made a U-turn on Crandon, heading toward home. With the car phone tucked on her shoulder, she punched in Vince's beeper number. She reached him on the third green at the Biltmore golf course. Obviously he wasn't worried about things back at the office. He figured carrying his cellular phone in his golf bag constituted working.

"What is it? I'm about to birdie this hole, Molly. Make it fast."

"I need to take the rest of the day off after all."

"Sure. Whatever," he muttered distractedly. He was probably on his knees sighting the curve of the green.

Molly started to hang up, when her words apparently registered.

"Hey, wait a second. Molly!"

She took her time responding, while he bellowed her name a few more times. "What?" she said finally.

"You'll be in tomorrow, though, right? We have that meeting at ten with the producer from Paramount. You have all the details."

She *always* had all the details. Vince's idea of being prepared consisted of putting the appointments on her calendar. "I could bring you up to speed just in case I can't make it," she suggested generously. "It wouldn't take more than a half hour or so." She enjoyed envisioning the ashen hue beneath Vince's tan as he measured the distance from ball to cup and saw the chance to play it out evaporating.

"No, no, I want you there. Gotta go, Molly." He hung up quickly, obviously afraid she might start briefing him right then and there.

As she turned into the palm-lined Ocean Manor entrance, she saw that police cars still filled the circular driveway in front of the gleaming white-and-glass building. Architecturally undistinctive, it was typical of dozens of beachfront condos along the Florida coast. Clean lines, light colors, classy if unimaginative decor.

Though she could have avoided the lobby, Molly took the main entrance just to see who was hanging around the murder scene. A small cluster of residents hovered near the security desk, as if being close to Nestor would protect them. The sight of the desk reminded Molly of something she should have considered much earlier. If anyone had come into the building last night, the name would be on the log, either at the desk or at the front gate. If the latter, a license tag number would have been recorded as well. She hoped the police hadn't already taken them as evidence.

While everyone was chatting, she inched closer to the desk and peered at the register. Tuesday's page was still on top. The last person to sign in had arrived at ten P.M., a Sylvia Machado, visiting Hector Alonso in 1020. There were no names after that. Anyone who'd arrived in the midst of this morning's confusion had slipped in unnoticed. Not even Nestor would have dared to make the police log in.

She was about to move away, when she realized that the gate log was also on the security desk. Obviously the guard had dropped it off before going off duty at seven. Again, Sylvia Machado was the last person registered, logged in at 9:55 P.M. It was possible that she was the killer and had lingered in the building until after the bridge game participants had gone to bed, but it seemed unlikely. It would be easy enough to check with Alonso to be sure that she'd been there as his guest.

Disappointed, Molly edged away from the desk. Jack Kingsley, the building manager, separated himself from another group near the bend in the corridor and met her in front of a scraggly potted palm that didn't appear to be in much better shape than Allan Winecroft.

Kingsley was a tall man, at least six-two, with a jovial round face and shrewd eyes. He looked to be about fifty. Bushy eyebrows sprinkled with gray tried to compensate for the thinning sandy hair on his head. Partial to the informal, open-necked guayabera shirts favored in the Latin community, he wore them with khaki trousers and boat shoes.

But while Kingsley's attire contributed to the impression that he was just about to head for a *café cubano* on Calle Ocho in the heart of Little Havana, word was that he ran a tight, businesslike ship. Molly had met him only twice, when she'd applied to the board for approval to buy her condo, and later when she'd gone to the office to make a maintenance payment. She'd been impressed, even a little intimidated by his odd balance of informal dress and militaristic regimentation. There was a lot of *yes, sir* and *no, sir* going on in that office. She'd been surprised that the secretaries hadn't snapped salutes.

"Mrs. DeWitt, could we talk a minute?" he asked her now. Without waiting for an answer, he steered her away from the crowd and toward the elevators. His pace was brisk. They were on their way to her apartment before she realized it. "I'm terribly sorry you've had to go through all of this," he said as he punched the button for the fifth floor. "I assume the police questioned you this morning."

"Some. They're going to want a formal statement later, I'm told."

"This is a terrible thing. Terrible. Do you have any idea what might have happened? Did you see anything at all?"

"Actually, no," she said, though she thought finding the body was quite enough. "Allan was fine when I left the cardroom last night."

"What time did you discover his body?"

"It must have been about eight."

"Had he been dead long?"

The question was natural enough, she supposed, but why ask her? She was no expert. The place was swarming with people likely to be better informed than she was. "I couldn't say. I'm sure the medical examiner will have to pin down the time of death. Is Allan . . . have they taken him away yet?"

"Yes. A few minutes ago. They've sealed off the cardroom for the time being. There are technicians all over the place in there and the detective in charge, Mr. O'Hara, I believe, said they'd want to speak with everyone."

"You mean those there last night?"

"No, he said everyone. I assured him we would make whatever arrangements he required. I've made up a list and set up a timetable, subject to his approval, of course. I'm expecting him back shortly."

Molly suddenly remembered something she'd

wondered about earlier as she'd surveyed the excep-
tionally tidy cardroom. "Mr. Kingsley, what time does
the cleaning staff get here?"

"Eight."

"So, there's no way they could have been in there
this morning?"

"You mean prior to your arrival?"

She nodded.

"It's not impossible. Occasionally the director of
housekeeping makes her rounds early before her staff
arrives. Why?"

"Because the room was spotless, except for Allan.
I wondered if they'd had time to pick up from last
night's bridge game."

"I doubt it. Even if Mrs. Rodriguez had been in,
she wouldn't have done the cleaning herself."

So, Molly thought, it was likely that the other players had cleaned up before leaving last night. Which of
them had remained behind to do it? Allan himself,
concerned about sticking to his own stringent rules?
Had he lingered, then been attacked by the killer, perhaps not a member of their own group, but a late
arrival he'd never even seen? He had been stabbed in
the back, after all. Or was it possible that the killer
himself had tidied up, worried about leaving behind
any evidence linking him to the crime? For that matter, was it possible that Allan had gone down this
morning to pick up something he'd left behind? Aside
from his clothes, she had no confirmation that he'd
been killed last night. Drucilla certainly hadn't noticed
that he'd been missing all night.

"Is there something more?" Mr. Kingsley asked,
regarding her curiously.

"No. I suppose not."

"Well, if there is anything I can do for you, you will let me know, won't you?" he said as they reached her door. "I remember what you told me about your reasons for leaving your house. I would hate to have you regret buying here. Ocean Manor needs more young, year-round owners."

Molly wondered if he feared a rush of sales. Were condos seriously affected by such signs of instability? For that matter, wouldn't a murder intimidate a lot of prospective buyers? Whatever his concerns, she sought to reassure him about her own plans. "I can't say I wasn't rattled when I discovered the body this morning, but I have no intention of being chased away, Mr. Kingsley." She paused. "You know, on second thought, you could tell me something else about Allan. Was he fully retired or did he still have business interests? Is there anything listed on the office records?"

"Why on earth would you ask something like that?" His expression was thoroughly puzzled.

"His wife mentioned that he'd stayed on last night to discuss business. I wondered if perhaps a deal had gone sour on him. Then, again, maybe it was just general financial chitchat."

"I'm sure that must have been it. Once you've been a CEO, the tendency to stay on top of things must always be there."

"Was Allan on top of what was happening here? I would think a man like that would make an excellent condominium president."

"He was very savvy."

Though the manager responded quickly, Molly

couldn't help thinking that there was more he wasn't saying. She recalled all those troubling rumors she'd heard and risked asking him about them. "I've heard there was some mismanagement by the old board. Is there any truth to that?"

"None at all," he said, again without hesitation. This time, though, he elaborated. "Condominiums are complex businesses. Not everyone understands all the intricacies. I'm sure that's why there was some confusion over decisions made in the past. Allan was brought up to speed on everything by the accountants. I think he was satisfied that everything was in order in the reports we showed him."

Molly nodded politely, but made a mental note to ask the accountants about that. "Good. I know how nervous people get when their money is at risk, and how rumors can take on a life of their own."

"Tell me about it. I've been managing condominiums in this state for the past twenty years. There's not a one of them that hasn't had its problems," he told her in confidence. "It's bound to happen when you get a few hundred owners with very different backgrounds all mixed together. We've got Cubans and South Americans, a few Germans, some Brits, plus all the retirees from up north and a handful of young professionals like yourself. No two of them has the same likes or the same expectations. Just try redecorating the corridors and you can end up with World War Three on your hands."

Molly could just imagine trying to get them all to agree on a color scheme, much less style or architectural alterations. "I'm sure," she said sympathetically.

"You just let Nestor or me know if you have any

problems," he said. "That's what we're here for. You get the shakes or anything from all this, give Dr. Meeks a call. I hear he's a pretty decent shrink."

"I'll do that," she said, though Roy Meeks was on her list of suspects and likely to be every bit as shaky as she was herself.

Comforted somewhat by the manager's solicitude, she made herself a tuna salad sandwich and took it onto her balcony overlooking a garden of sea grapes and beyond that the beach and ocean. The temperature had climbed into the low eighties and the humidity was high. Only a breeze kept it from being unbearable. It was still the perfect place to collect her thoughts. It reminded her of carefree summer days on her front porch overlooking the Rappahannock in Virginia. She'd spent endless hours on that porch daydreaming and making plans.

Today, though, there was no time for daydreams. If anything, she was in the middle of a nightmare. Leaving the sandwich untouched, she began making a list of those she wanted to see: the Davisons, Tyler Jenkins and his wife, Roy Meeks. She'd have to ask them to identify some of the others who'd been there last night. She considered asking them all over for tea despite O'Hara's objections. Tapping her pen against the table, she tried to imagine anyone making incriminating revelations under those conditions. It wouldn't happen. She'd have to approach them one by one. Divide and conquer. The phrase suddenly held new meaning.

Before she could pick her first target, though, the phone rang. She ran inside, but when she picked up the phone, there was no answer on the other end.

"Hello," she repeated. "Is someone there? Hello!"

The only response was a soft click.

"A wrong number," she murmured, walking slowly back to the balcony. Something deep in her gut, however, told her she was wrong. She couldn't help remembering what Drucilla had said earlier. Allan had been receiving threatening phone calls before he was killed. As dark clouds rolled in, warning of the impending onset of the typical afternoon thunderstorms, she shivered in the sudden gloom. She picked up her notes and sandwich and took them inside.

In the kitchen, she glanced at her list and decided the place to start would be with the man who'd championed Allan's election to the board, the man Drucilla so clearly resented: Tyler Jenkins.

Despite the threatening weather, she found Tyler walking laps around the perimeter of the pool, looking dapper in a crisp short-sleeved cotton shirt and shorts that displayed his knobby knees. His leather sneakers still looked brand-new. Apparently this was a recent regimen, probably prescribed after his bypass.

Molly smiled a greeting, which drew only a cursory nod and a terse, "Mrs. DeWitt."

"Mind if I join you?"

He stopped and studied her, his suspicious blue eyes intent. "Why?"

"I'd like to talk to you a little about Allan, if I could."

"The man's dead," he said, resuming his pace. "No point in talking about him."

"He was a friend of yours. I'm sure this has been a terrible shock."

"Damned fool," he muttered.

Molly wasn't sure if he was referring to Allan or to her. "Why would you say that?" she asked.

He waved aside the question. "Don't mind me. You're right. This has been a shock."

"Drucilla says you worked very hard to get Allan on the board."

"Thought he'd be good. Not like all those others who were greedy and power hungry. Man had business sense. Ran a huge corporation. This should have been a piece of cake for him."

"Should have been? Wasn't it?"

"Different kettle of fish altogether, he told me. Might have been president, but he wasn't really in charge. Board outvoted him at every turn. Should have thought of that," he said, stepping up his pace until Molly practically had to run to keep up with him. For a man still recuperating from surgery, he seemed awfully fit to her.

Molly was also having some difficulty in reconciling the image of Allan as kindly businessman out to do good with the petty tyrant he'd appeared to be to others. The sheet of rules, circulated less than a week ago, came to mind as did a few incidents she'd heard about.

"Wasn't there a suit of some sort?" she asked. "Something about a cat?"

Faded blue eyes snapping with indignation glowered at her. "A lot of damned nonsense," Tyler decreed. "Can't have animals roving all over the place. The rules are clear. No pets. Allan was just enforcing them."

"But as I understand it, Mrs. Jenko had owned

that cat for nearly fourteen years. She brought it with
her when she moved in. No one told her she couldn't.
Besides, it never left her apartment. What possible difference could it make if she kept it?''

"A rule's a rule. Can't have exceptions. Leads to
chaos."

Molly was beginning to get an idea of where Allan
had gotten his notions about condo law and order.
Tyler Jenkins was a crotchety old man. He'd probably
instigated the incident over the Firths' child being
barefoot in the lobby. Liza Hastings, who lived across
the hall from Molly, had told her all about it. Four
adults—the Firths, Allan, and Tyler—had stood in the
middle of the lobby shouting, while two-year-old Hettie Firth screamed, probably in a rage over being sin-
gled out for her tiny bare feet. It had taken Nestor and
another guard to calm things down.

"Mr. Jenkins, Drucilla seems to think that Allan
was being threatened because of something he'd done
as condo president. Is that possible?"

"World's a terrible place when a man's con-
demned for just doing his job."

"Does that mean yes?"

"Wouldn't surprise me. That guard threatened
him. He's probably the one. That policeman won't go
after one of his own, though."

It took Molly several minutes to figure out what
Tyler meant. The guard in question, Enrique Valdez,
had been fired over some incident at the front gate.
He'd admitted someone without noting it in the log.
The guest happened to be visiting Allan. Allan had
fired Enrique, setting off a barrage of criticism from

those who thought he should have been given a second chance.

"Have you told Detective O'Hara about the incident?"

"Haven't seen him. Doubt he'll listen, though. Those Cubans protect each other. That's a fact."

Molly refrained from offering her own observation about the detective's impartiality. He liked her—at least she thought he did—and that wasn't keeping him from putting her on his list of suspects.

"Did Allan suggest that Enrique was making those calls?"

"No."

"Did he mention what the calls were about?"

"Said they were a damned nuisance, no more than that."

"So he wasn't frightened?"

"Take more than an anonymous call or two to scare a man like Allan."

Molly wasn't so sure about that. It had taken only one hang-up to make her jittery. She was about to comment on that when Michael O'Hara himself fell into stride beside them. She doubted he was there for the exercise.

"Is this a private conversation or can anyone join in?" he inquired. His expression indicated that any hint of exclusivity would not be appreciated.

The old man's eyes narrowed. "You that cop?"

"Michael O'Hara."

Tyler looked as if he'd been offered a dose of castor oil. "Time for my nap."

"I'm afraid your nap will have to wait for a few more minutes," Michael said, following him as he headed toward the building. Molly stayed in stride partly out of habit, but mostly out of curiosity. Why was Tyler Jenkins so afraid of talking to the police?

"Doctor says I have to rest. Can't change the schedule."

This from a man who'd just done twenty laps around a very large pool at a pace just under a trot. Molly had her doubts. Apparently Michael did as well. His determination never faltered. "Perhaps if we sit here in the shade," he suggested.

Still grumbling under his breath, Mr. Jenkins sat. Michael sat opposite him. Molly lingered hopefully.

"Sit," Michael said finally. She pulled up a chair before he could change his mind.

"Mr. Jenkins, tell me about your relationship with Allan Winecroft. Was he a protégé of yours?"

"Got him to run for the board, if that's what you mean. Saw that he got elected."

"You must have a lot of influence in the building then."

"Some."

"Why didn't you run yourself?"

"Bad heart. Doc said I couldn't take it."

That hadn't kept him from running a vitriolic campaign, however. Molly had read some of his campaign letters on Allan's behalf. The Republican National Committee couldn't have taken nastier potshots at the Democrats.

"Once he was elected, was he panning out the way you'd hoped he would?" Michael asked.

"He was tough. Given the chance, he would have made a damned fine president."

"Any idea who might not have wanted him to have that chance?"

"Always a few malcontents. Doubt they'd have killed him, though."

"Why not let me be the judge of that? I'd like their names anyway."

"Talk to Manuel Mendoza."

"Who is he?"

"He's the man Allan beat in the last election. Thought he had a lock on the position. Damned Latin coalition. Always talking Spanish in the elevators. Wouldn't know we're still in America, if they had their way."

Even though there was no sign of a reaction on Michael's face, Molly winced. She'd heard Tyler Jenkins's frustration from an increasing number of Anglos as the Hispanic population began to dominate the county. Apparently Tyler didn't care that the man he was talking to was also Hispanic. Nor was he worried about sharing the depth of his bitterness over the community's changes.

No doubt Michael had heard similar complaints before. Ignoring the prejudiced comment with admirable restraint, he asked, "Mr. Jenkins, where were you between midnight and eight this morning?"

The old man didn't even blink. "In my apartment."

"Anyone with you?"

"My wife. She'll tell you I never left."

Michael closed his notebook. "Yes. I'm sure she will. And she was at the bridge game as well, is that right?"

"Yes. We play every Tuesday. Won last year."

"Congratulations and thank you for your time, sir." He stood up and gestured to Molly. From the stern expression on his face again, she decided it wouldn't be wise to argue.

Before he could launch into a tirade, she said, "I got a call this afternoon. I wasn't going to say anything, but maybe you should know about it."

"What sort of call?"

"A hang-up, but I could tell someone was there at first. I'm sure it was nothing, probably just a wrong number. I mean no one would expect me to be home this time of day, right?"

"Did anyone see you come in?"

"Yes," she admitted. "There were at least a dozen people in the lobby."

"Any of the people who were playing cards last night?"

She tried to recall if she'd seen anyone she recognized. "No," she said finally. "Other than the guards and the manager, they weren't people I knew."

He nodded. "Did the call upset you for some particular reason?"

"No. Not really. It's just that I went through something like this a few years ago. It gave me a start to have it happen again."

"It was probably nothing, but let me know if you get another call, okay?" He took a card out of his shirt pocket and jotted a number on the back. "Call anytime. My home number's on the back."

"Why was I less nervous before I told you?"

"Because I'm taking it seriously?" he suggested. "I have to. In situations like this it's never smart to overlook anything. I tend not to believe in coincidence. You have a cute kid to worry about, too. It might have been nothing more than a wrong number, but don't take any foolish chances if it happens again. Call."

Molly nodded.

"And one more thing," he said, his tone light. It contradicted the cold look back in his eyes. "Stay away from the other suspects. Finding you with them is really getting on my nerves."

"Maybe you ought to be quicker," she said, then wished she hadn't. Michael O'Hara was definitely not in any mood for jokes. If anything, he looked like someone who was only a frayed strand of self-control away from throttling her.

CHAPTER
FIVE

For all of Tyler's obvious bias in bringing up Enrique Valdez as a suspect in the first place, Molly couldn't help wondering if the security guard had harbored a grudge against Allan. It would have been natural under the circumstances. For that matter, what about Violet Jenko? Since the elderly resident was essentially housebound, Molly decided to stop by her apartment en route to her own. A social call, in case Detective O'Hara asked.

Molly tapped loudly on the door of the first-floor apartment and waited patiently. Mrs. Jenko was both hard of hearing and required the use of a walker to get around. The combination slowed her down. Finally Molly heard the soft thud of rubber against tile as Mrs. Jenko neared the door.

"Who's there?" she said, her voice clear and sharp.

"It's Molly DeWitt, Mrs. Jenko, from upstairs."

She spoke loudly enough to be heard over the argument on *Geraldo*.

The door opened a cautious crack, revealing a frail, bent woman with flyaway wisps of white hair. She was wearing a flowered housecoat and fuzzy pink slippers. Assured that it was indeed Molly, she removed the chain and opened the door wide. She waved Molly inside, then replaced the deadbolt and the chain.

"Would you like some tea?" she offered, obviously glad of the unexpected company.

"I would love some," Molly said, adapting her steps to Mrs. Jenko's slow progress into the kitchen. "Could I help?"

"What's that?"

Molly raised her voice. "Do you need any help?"

"No need. Just sit there at the table. This won't take a minute."

The walker thumped across the tiles as she moved from sink to stove to cupboards. The room had been painted a bright sunshine-yellow once, but the color had dimmed with grease and time. Maybe Mrs. Jenko couldn't see all that well to clean.

The elderly woman carefully placed two English bone china teacups on the table. Next she brought over a plate with wedges of Scottish shortbread, the kind made with enough butter to clog the heartiest arteries. Molly loved it. She was just sorry there were only four pieces on the plate. When the tea had been poured and she'd taken her first sip, Molly said, "How are you doing, Mrs. Jenko? Have you been getting out at all?"

"What's that?"

"Have you been out?"

"Just to the mailbox. That takes most of the afternoon," she said wearily. "Can't move the way I used to. Why, when I was a girl . . ."

Sensing the start of a long session of reminiscences, Molly interrupted. "You haven't been too upset over Mr. Winecroft's murder, have you? Are you nervous being here alone?"

"Doesn't have a thing in the world to do with me," she said adamantly, thumping her walker for emphasis. "The man deserved to die."

"Because of that suit you had over your cat?"

Her nut-brown eyes misted over. "It was a cruel thing, what he did. Prissy was all I had in this world. She barely made a sound, never even left the apartment."

"How did he know about her then?"

"That hateful Tyler Jenkins told him. Tyler used to come nosing around, pretending to be concerned about how I was doing. He knew what that cat meant to me, but he told Allan about her anyway. Next thing I knew I was told Prissy had to go. I fought it as long as I could, but my son finally insisted I stop. Said it wasn't good for my blood pressure. Wish I had dropped dead. Then we really would have had a claim against the old coot."

"You don't mean that."

"Course I do. You think it's any fun living like this? Might as well be dead. Only thing worth staying alive for was seeing Allan Winecroft with that knife sticking out of him."

"You saw him?"

"You bet. The minute I heard the news. Went

right over there to see for myself that someone had done him in.''

"Any idea who?"

"No, but if I did, I'd surely thank them.''

Molly finally excused herself and left, after seeing Mrs. Jenko settled in the living room again, her television tuned to the early evening news. The sound followed her all the way down the hall. Her talk with the old woman had confirmed the depth of the bitter feud she'd had with Allan, but it also had proved, to Molly at least, that she wasn't capable of plunging that knife herself. She wouldn't have had the strength for it.

Enrique, on the other hand, was a powerfully built man. Molly spent an hour trying to track him down, to no avail. His wife claimed he was working somewhere as a painter. She had no idea where. Her grasp of English conveniently faded in and out. Molly left a message, but she wasn't surprised that Enrique never returned the call. She went to bed every bit as confused as she had been when she'd discovered Allan's body that morning.

• • •

Once Molly dropped Brian off at school in the morning, she turned automatically into Harbor Plaza Shopping Center. Down at the end, an *R* missing from its restaurant sign on the overhang, was the Doughnut Gallery, or the DG, as it was fondly known by the regulars. Long and narrow, the place was an island institution, its back wall decorated with snapshots of customers. Even the *Miami Herald* knew to send its reporters here when it wanted the latest word on Key Biscayne happenings.

Naturally, this morning the talk at the crowded counter centered on the Allan Winecroft murder. As she waited for a seat to open up, Molly listened as two other condo presidents worried aloud. They were less concerned with Allan's fate than with the possibility that their own lives might be at stake.

"You should have heard that guy last week, when the board turned down his renters," Jacob Gelbman said as the waitress set his daily breakfast of juice, cereal and a banana in front of him. He was so nervous he nearly poured his juice on his corn flakes. "He threatened to get us all for depriving him of his livelihood. I sympathized with the guy, but I couldn't vote to let the prospective tenant in. He had too many kids for a two-bedroom apartment. The owner was furious, practically turned purple, said we were ruining him."

"That's just talk," George Calhoun retorted, going against medical guidelines to douse his scrambled eggs with salt. He picked up a piece of crisp bacon in his fingers and waved it between bites. "If I had a nickel for all the threats made against our condo board, I'd be a rich man."

"You are a rich man," Gelbman reminded him. "Maybe you and I can afford to take a few knocks. What if this guy in our building couldn't? What if he goes berserk like that guy up in Broward County last year? He allegedly shot the condo president, then went home and had a drink. That's where they found him, out by his pool, a drink in his hand, calm as you please. Desperation makes people do crazy things. Now this thing with Winecroft. Who knows what's behind that? I tell you, I'm thinking of getting off the board. Let somebody else take the heat. What do you get for doing it? A lot of aggravation. That's it. Nothing but aggravation."

A stool opened up next to Gelbman. Molly squeezed onto it, nodding to the men. She knew them the way she knew all of the regulars, by name and condo. She knew very little about their backgrounds, though both appeared to be retirement age. Gelbman had thinning white hair and nervous mannerisms even when he wasn't contemplating a murder. Calhoun had the tanned, leathery skin of a man who couldn't stay away from the beach or the golf course. They were always together and always here when she arrived.

Before she could blink, her cup of coffee was in front of her, along with the skim milk for her high-fiber cereal. If she ever wanted to change her order, she'd have to shout it from the doorway. Once she was seated, her usual breakfast materialized automatically. There was something especially comforting about that routine this morning.

"What do you think, Molly?" Jacob Gelbman asked. "You live in the building. Was it one of the owners who stabbed Winecroft? There's always some brouhaha going on over there. Maybe one of 'em turned nasty."

"I have no idea who did it," she said honestly. Nothing she'd done so far had narrowed down her initial list of suspects, much less added anyone to it. Despite her desire to dig for more clues, she'd spent the previous evening helping Brian with his homework after her visit to Violet Jenko. Though on the surface Brian was nonchalant about the murder, she'd sensed a vague tension in him that she attributed to unspoken fears. She hadn't tried to force him to talk, but she had remained available to listen. He'd spent most of the evening talking about snakes and what terrific pets they made. She'd shuddered at the very idea. Thank goodness the rules forbade it.

"But the paper says you discovered the body," Gelbman protested. "Surely you have some theories about what happened."

"I found Allan's body, but unfortunately the killer didn't linger with it. Your guess is as good as mine." She patted herself on the back for remaining dutifully neutral. Detective O'Hara would be proud of her. Just to be sure she kept her opinions to herself, she stuffed a spoonful of bran flakes into her mouth.

"I heard there were a lot of bitter feelings after the last election, though. Who was that guy who ran against Winecroft and lost?"

"Manuel Mendoza," Molly said, recalling that Tyler Jenkins had raised the same possibility.

"Right. That's it. Mendoza. Maybe he's still holding a grudge."

"The election was eight months ago," she reminded them. "If you ask me, he ought to be relieved he lost. The board has been catching flak from the owners from the minute they took office. They're fighting over the assessments. They're fighting over cable TV. They're fighting over the decorating. When those cheap lighting fixtures went up in the halls, I thought Miriam Powell was going to have a fit of apoplexy. She said the property value was going to be ruined. I don't think that makes her a murderer."

"But you can't say that for sure. You've got three hundred apartments, right? Every owner's taste is different. You try pleasing them all. It can't be done. Not a day goes by that someone's not mad at you. If the police are on top of this, that's where they'll start looking, at the board minutes. See who was griping about what. Maybe somebody tried to sell and the deal wasn't approved by the board. Could be the seller was real anxious. Or maybe the buyer resented being turned down. That's the place to start, in the minutes."

"Good idea." The approving comment came from behind the newspaper to Molly's right. Already it was a familiar voice.

She nabbed a corner of the paper and folded it down until she could peer straight into Detective O'Hara's eyes. "It is not polite to eavesdrop."

"It's worse than that to defy a direct police order."

"I'm not defying anything. I'm eating my breakfast." She waved a spoonful of now soggy flakes in his direction.

"But the name Allan Winecroft did cross your lips, did it not?"

"Not mine, theirs."

"A technicality."

Both men on her left suddenly seemed totally absorbed with stirring their coffee. Molly recognized an evasion tactic when she saw one. Neither man used sugar. Or cream. Unless one of them had switched to tea and was trying to change his fortune in the leaves, they were trying to avoid the detective's attention. Since they'd dragged her into this conversation, she saw no reason to hang alone.

"Gentlemen, I'd like you to meet Detective O'Hara. He's in charge of the Winecroft investigation. Perhaps he can answer your questions. I have to go to work." She slid off the stool and grabbed for her check in one fluid motion. Even if it hadn't been there, she knew the amount by heart. It never changed.

"Oh, no, you don't," the detective said, snagging her wrist and holding her in place. "I heard something last night that might interest you."

The entire restaurant was not much bigger than her living room, just the right size for spreading gossip. A definite stillness fell over the row of diners. The only sounds were the sizzle of eggs on the grill and toast popping up. Michael was quick enough to pick up on the sudden fascination with their conversation.

"Not here," he said, snatching his own check off the counter and steering her down the narrow aisle toward the door. He barely paused at the cashier to hand over a fistful of bills. "Hers, too," he said.

"I'll pay for my own breakfast."

"It's already done," he muttered, nudging her toward the door. Molly barely had time to grab the cup of coffee she always ordered to go. It was thrust into her hand just as she scooted out the door.

When they were outside, Molly jerked her arm out of his grip and demanded, "Were you in there spying on me?"

"I was in there for toast and coffee."

"Right." She wondered exactly how long he'd lingered over refills of the coffee. The place had been open since five thirty. Unless he drank decaf, by now he ought to be wired for the day. She wasn't about to risk tangling with a man whose nerves were jittery and who carried a gun. She kept a lid on any further sarcastic observations. She couldn't help it, though, if her expression remained skeptical.

"Okay," he muttered finally. "Maybe I thought I could pick up on a little local gossip, see if Allan was beloved or hated. I'm well aware that half the movers and shakers on the island stop in there for breakfast." He slammed his fist against the roof of his Jeep. "Damn! Why am I explaining myself to you?"

"Guilt," she suggested.

"Not a word you should be throwing around under the circumstances."

"What is that supposed to mean?"

"Word has it that Allan recently had a set-to with your son. The person who mentioned this suggested that you are a very protective mother."

Molly regarded him incredulously. "What exactly was this set-to supposed to be about?"

"The informant seemed a little vague on that."

"I'm sure. It never happened, Detective. Brian would never argue with an adult."

This time the detective looked skeptical. Obviously interrogating witnesses gave him a lot of practice.

"Okay," she agreed. "He can be a little sassy, but that's with me. He's been taught to respect his elders. Besides, he would have told me if Allan had been on his case over something."

"That's the point. He told you. You got huffy and stabbed the man. At least that's the theory."

"Yours or the informant's?"

"The informant's."

"Good, because I'd hate to think you were that stupid."

"Not stupid, just thorough. I have to check out everything."

Maybe he was just being cautious. Or maybe he'd been taken for a ride once and vowed never to trust his own judgment again. Molly preferred those theories to the one giving him one more item to add to her own list of motives. "Did some sweet-talking person fool you once? Did she mess up a case for you?"

"Nope, and that's not going happen if I can help it. When it comes to a case, I don't trust my parish priest. Now that we're clear this isn't personal, let's stick to the specifics of this case. You're saying the incident between Allan and Brian never happened?"

"That's right. It never happened."

"Could we talk to your son about that?"

"Why? I've told you."

"And I'm trying to cover all the bases."

She glared at him. His gaze met hers evenly, unfazed by the scowl. There was enough chemistry in the air to blow up a lab. For once it didn't have much to do with physical attraction. She was furious, resentful of the fact he wouldn't take her at her word. He was patient, which only magnified her irritation.

"He's at school," she said finally.

"Later, then. I'll stop by this evening."

"Whatever," she said stiffly.

"Thank you," he said formally, a glimmer of amusement in his eyes.

She relented. He was just trying to do his job. "By the way, what was the consensus in there this morning?" she asked. "Was Allan loved or hated?"

"Actually, it was odd. Everyone had something to say about the murder, but very little about Allan. Except for the condo, did he pretty much keep to himself?"

"He played tennis, but those guys are already on the courts by now. Other than that I have no idea if he'd involved himself in any of the other island activities. Try the Yacht Club or check with *The Islander*. Someone at the paper might know if he was active."

"Maybe I'll just drop in on his wife, instead."

There was an unmistakable spark of anticipation in his voice. "You're hoping she'll have company, right?"

"I must admit to a certain curiosity about who was expected yesterday. A lover, especially one interested in her husband's estate, might have a particularly good motive for stabbing Allan."

If Molly hadn't had that damned meeting with Paramount, she might very well have begged to tag along. Instead, she drove to work at a daring ten miles an hour above the speed limit. Despite her defiance of the traffic laws, she still had to stay in the slow lane to avoid being run down by everyone else. Where the hell was a cop when you really needed one?

CHAPTER
SIX

When Molly arrived at the office, Vince and Jeannette were in the midst of a standoff. For the second time that morning she was grateful that the world around her was still so normal.

"What are you two bickering about now?" she asked as she inched between two floor-to-tabletop stacks of *Variety,* the *Hollywood Reporter,* tourism brochures, and magazines to reach her desk.

Jeannette, a tall, stately black woman with close-cropped hair, rolled her expressive eyes and launched into a soft but eloquent tirade in Creole. There was just enough English to give Molly the idea that Vince had been behaving in character. Apparently he recognized the phrase that meant son of a bitch as well. He dragged Molly into his office and slammed the door, leaving an indignant Jeannette on the other side.

"I can't deal with this," he said. "I've had it."

"What's the problem?"

"She refuses to do the filing."

"Did she say that?"

"Well, not in so many words," he admitted, "but do you see any sign of her doing it? She's just muttering all that voodoo stuff again."

"What on earth makes you think she's invoking some curse?"

"It's the way she looks at me. Gives me the chills."

"Perhaps she looks like that because you're behaving like a jerk. I've occasionally felt a need to regard you that way myself. Look, I'll talk to her. We'll get caught up on the filing. Maybe if the phone didn't ring off the hook around here, she'd have time to do it."

"It's not my fault that they eliminated a secretarial position."

"Nobody said it was. We just have to do the best we can. Have a cup of coffee. Go over your notes for the Paramount meeting. Daydream about your golf game. Did you make that birdie, by the way?"

"Now that," he said with a satisfied sigh, all thoughts of Jeannette banished in a wave of pure nostalgia, "that was perfection. You should have been there, Molly. A fifteen-footer, straight into the cup."

"Did you win?"

"Naw, but who cares? Came in six over par, the best I've played in months. I'm telling you, if I could hit the course every day I could turn pro."

"Vince, by the time you're ready for that you'll have to go on the seniors tour. Stick with the amateur stuff. Now let me go see if I can calm Jeannette down."

She found the clerk diligently filing. Jeannette glanced up, a twinkle in her dark-brown eyes.

"Okay, tell the truth, what'd you say to him?" Molly asked.

"I wished him many children," she said innocently.

Molly chuckled. "So he was right. You did put a curse on him."

A grin spread slowly across Jeannette's flat features, her white teeth gleaming against a mahogany complexion. "He would see it that way, yes."

"Jeannette, one of these days he's going to fire you. Why can't you just talk to him in plain English? You speak it every bit as well as I do."

"But what would be the fun in that? Vincent, he has an idea of who I am. Why should I distress him by confusing the matter?"

"I have a pretty good idea of who you are, too, my friend, and you are a fraud. You have more business and political savvy than Vince would if he got an MBA. Don't let him sell you short."

"This is a clerk's job, Molly. If he sees I am over-qualified, it will make him very nervous. I watch the county listings. When a better job comes along, I will apply. Until then I will do this one well, even the filing." Her grin was back. "And have a little fun, yes?"

Molly chuckled. "Okay, yes."

Jeannette's expression sobered. "Now we talk about you. You are okay? I saw in the paper about the murder in your building."

"I'm okay. I just wish I could figure out who was behind it. It makes me very nervous to think that someone in Ocean Manor is capable of murder. That means they have access to all the apartments."

As Jeannette went back to her filing, Molly considered the suspects who had surfaced thus far: Drucilla, Manuel Mendoza, perhaps Tyler Jenkins, the fired Enrique Valdez, some unidentified and possibly nonexistent lover of Drucilla's, some of the others who'd been there last night. She excluded herself for obvious reasons. She knew she hadn't done it. If the police had a more solid list, weeding out the unlikeliest prospects, she wasn't aware of it.

She glanced at her watch. She had about ten minutes before the meeting with the Paramount producer. That ought to be just about long enough for a chat with Mendoza. She looked up the number of his development company in Coral Gables.

To reach him she had to convince a receptionist and then a secretary that her business with him was important. Fortunately, dealing with Hollywood office help had given her the necessary skills to bluff her way past the most protective executive secretaries.

"Mr. Mendoza, this is Molly DeWitt. I live at Ocean Manor."

"Right. Right. You're the one who discovered Allan's body, right?"

"Yes. I was wondering if you might tell me a little bit about condo politics. I'm new to the building and I'm wondering how Allan got elected."

Although Mendoza had been speaking perfectly fluent, unaccented English, her question brought on a barrage of Spanish.

"You didn't like him, I take it."

"He was an interloper."

"What an odd choice of words. Hadn't he lived in the building for many years?"

"A few, but only recently did he become interested in power."

"Perhaps that was because of some of the concerns about mismanagement I've heard."

"You have been misinformed. The building has been run very well," he said coldly. "I have seen to that. Now, if you'll excuse me, I am very busy."

"Wait," Molly said, anxious for a more definitive explanation.

"Good-bye, Mrs. DeWitt."

Manuel Mendoza's abrupt end to their conversation stayed with her throughout the meeting with the producers from Los Angeles. Had the ex–condo president interpreted her comment as an accusation? Had guilt made him anxious to be rid of her? Mendoza had been president of the board for three terms, and it was during that time that suggestions of impropriety had been raised. If someone had been offering sweetheart deals to contractors, who better to do it than a developer? Allan's election would have brought an unwanted close to a lucrative side business. Was there enough at stake to justify killing him to pave the way for a new election? And how did Jack Kingsley fit in? Wouldn't the manager have to know what was going on?

When she got home that afternoon she went straight to the office and asked to see copies of the most recent budgets. Mr. Kingsley emerged from his office just as the reports were being handed to her.

"What brings you in?" he asked, taking the papers from Celia before Molly could get her hands on them. He glanced through them, then passed them on. Reluctantly? Molly couldn't be sure.

"I thought I'd try to catch up on what goes on around here," she said, tucking the papers into her briefcase before he could change his mind. "I wasn't here when the budget was approved. I have no idea how a place like this operates. If I'm going to pay a thousand dollars every quarter for maintenance, I want to see how it's spent."

"Very prudent," he agreed. "Celia, get her the proposed budget as well as last year's actuals."

The petite blonde bobbed her head. "Should I get the report that just came in from . . ."

"No, that won't be necessary."

"Which report is that?" Molly asked. "Everything is a matter of public record, isn't it?"

"Once it's been presented to the board, naturally."

"I see. Then this report Celia mentioned hasn't gone to the board yet?"

"It's on the agenda for next week. Of course, with all that's happened, the timetable could be shifted. I imagine most of the meeting will be devoted to replacing Allan."

"The bylaws call for another election, isn't that right?"

"Yes. He had most of his term remaining, so there will need to be a new election, rather than an appointment."

"Any idea who might run?"

"Mendoza's the most likely candidate. Has all sorts of experience from before. He could move right in and know what needs to be done."

She nodded. "Yes. I'm sure that's important." She

stepped to the door. "Well, thanks for these, Celia. Good-bye, Mr. Kingsley."

He nodded. Before she'd taken two steps down the hall, however, she could hear his raised voice. She got the distinct impression he wasn't happy with Celia's generosity with the building's budget figures.

When Michael showed up a half hour later, she was still going over the two reports. Although in some areas the costs seemed high, she couldn't find any obvious discrepancies. Not that she knew what to look for. Obviously the figures were going to add up. The only way to find really lousy deals would be to see comparative bids on everything.

"What do you have there?" Michael asked, glancing at the papers she'd spread out on the coffee table. "You bring some work home?"

"No. Actually, it's the condo budget."

He groaned. "I don't suppose it just happened to be in the mail today."

"No. I asked for it. It seems to me that . . ."

"Dammit, woman, haven't you heard a single thing I've said to you?"

She gazed at him innocently. "Which things were those?"

"Let me narrow it down to one." He leaned in close. "Stay out of this case."

"Hey, you're the one who put me on the list of suspects."

"But we both know you don't belong there."

Surprised to hear him actually say it, she said, "Thank you. When did you decide that?"

"I've never believed you are capable of murder. However, someone is taking great pains to make me believe you are, starting with using your knife, making sure only your prints were on it, and then telling me about a set-to between you and Allan over your boy. Hasn't it occurred to you that someone, possibly the killer, is very anxious to see you behind bars? If it is the killer and if he or she decides that the tactic isn't working, it may seem to him or her that more drastic measures are called for.''

With all those *him*s and *her*s and *someone*s scattered around, it was tricky, but Molly was relatively certain she understood what he was getting at. In fact, the picture he was painting made her blood run cold. Just in case she'd got it wrong, she asked, "Meaning?"

"Meaning, dammit, that you could be in danger. Now will you just stay the hell out of my way!"

She was ninety-nine percent certain that it wasn't a question. "Okay, yes. I'll back off. I still think there might be information I could get for you . . ."

"As a detective I have access to more information than you could possibly imagine."

"But people might be more open with me."

Wiping his hand wearily across his face, he sat down. "Okay, let's just suppose for a minute that you do get someone to spill his guts. Then you'd have exactly the information the killer is trying to keep us from getting. Talk about a motive for murder."

"Okay, okay, I get your point."

"Is Brian home?"

"Yes. He's in his room."

"Get him, please."

His temper appeared to be on a very short leash. Molly went to get Brian. Naturally, he wasn't in his room. He was standing in the shadows just beyond the

living room. He'd obviously heard every word. For the
first time since the murder, he looked scared. When
she gestured for him to come, he hung back.

"What did he mean, Mom? Is somebody going to
hurt you?"

"No, Brian. You and I are going to look out for
each other, and we'll be just fine."

"Maybe Detective O'Hara ought to look out for
us. He has a gun."

"We're not going to need a gun. Come on, kiddo.
The detective has a couple of questions for you."

For once the prospect of being a part of the investigation didn't seem to appeal to him. He stayed right
where he was.

"Brian, what on earth is wrong? He just needs to
ask you a couple of questions."

"I don't know anything, not really."

The *not really* worried her. That generally meant
he knew something but didn't deem it important according to his own value system. His system quite often
varied considerably from those of such authority figures as his mother and his teachers.

"I want you in the living room right now, and I
want you to answer every question Detective O'Hara
asks with the truth. Do you understand me?"

"Yes, ma'am," he said dutifully, but he didn't look
happy about it. She recognized that stubborn set of his
mouth and wondered how the detective would do at
getting past it.

Michael looked up from the budget papers and
smiled at Brian. "Hey, *amigo,* how's it going?"

"Okay, I guess," Brian said, leaning against
Molly's knee.

"I need your help."

"My help?" he said, straightening a little. "What can I do? I'm just a kid."

"I need to know if you ever saw Mr. Winecroft around the building."

Apparently Brian thought the question was innocuous enough. He responded readily. "Sure. He was always around."

"Did you ever talk to him?"

"Not much. I don't think he liked kids very much."

"What made you think that?"

"He was always yelling at us."

"Us? You and who else?"

"Timmy and Kevin. We'd swim every afternoon. Sometimes we'd go to the beach and forget to wash the sand off our feet before we went into the pool or we'd sit on one of the chairs without a towel."

"Did he yell at you recently?"

Brian glanced at Molly uneasily. "Yeah, I guess."

"How recently?"

"Day before yesterday."

"What were you doing then?"

"Nothing, not really. We were in the garage, see, just messing around. We weren't hurting anything. And he caught us. He said he was going to call the police if he saw us near there again." His lower lip quivered and Molly could see the sheen of tears welling up in his eyes.

"Near where?"

"I don't know. That was the really weird part. I mean we were just sort of hiding and stuff."

"Was he alone or was someone with him?"

"I didn't see anybody."

"Could you show me where you were?"

Sensing finally that he wasn't in any real trouble, Brian's expression brightened. "Sure."

Michael nodded. "Let's go take a look."

The building's garage was on a single level, beneath the structure but aboveground. Outside light filtered in, but it was the overhead fluorescent lights that kept it from being gloomy. Unlike some dark, shadowy parking garages that scared Molly to death, she'd never felt anything but safe in this one. Until now. There was something about Brian's story that suggested that something had been happening in the garage that Allan Winecroft hadn't wanted anyone to know about.

Brian led them to the area near the greenhouse along the outside perimeter of the garage. The building's plants were brought here to recuperate. The area was filled now with a few small potted palms and trays of impatiens and two or three plastic sacks of potting soil. As far as Molly could see there was nothing sinister going on.

"Was this the way it looked when you saw Mr. Winecroft here?" Michael asked.

"I guess," Brian said slowly. "We weren't even in the greenhouse part."

Molly noticed the nearby hoses, kept there both to water the plants and for resident use in washing their cars. "You weren't spraying each other with the hoses, were you?"

"Not exactly."

"Either you were or you weren't."

Brian scuffed the toe of his sneaker along the cement. "Maybe just a little. It was really hot that day."

"You had an entire ocean and a pool, if you wanted to cool off."

Brian looked subdued.

"Were you getting water on the cars?"

"Maybe some of them," he admitted.

"Is that why Mr. Winecroft got mad?"

"Maybe. I guess."

Molly and Michael exchanged a look. "So much for that," she said.

Michael nodded. "Maybe."

"You think it was something else?"

"I'm not sure. I just can't imagine him getting all worked up over a couple of cars getting sprayed."

"Maybe one of them was his."

"So what? All he had to do was ask the kids to dry it off. Remember what I was told, that he'd been so furious with Brian that you'd gotten even by stabbing him to death."

"How mad was he, Brian?"

"Pretty mad. He was really yelling and stuff. He turned real red. He even said he'd have us all kicked out. I was gonna tell you, Mom, but I forgot."

"More likely you figured I'd punish you."

"Not really, because we didn't *do* anything. Not anything bad."

Allan Winecroft apparently hadn't seen it that way. Was it possible that Brian had seen something and just hadn't realized it? She could tell from the speculative gleam in Michael's eyes that he was thinking the same thing.

"Did I help?" Brian asked.

"Yes," Michael said slowly. "Yes, I think you did."

As they started back toward the building, Molly heard a faint scrambling sound, a slight rustling. Michael and Brian apparently heard it too. They all looked back toward the greenhouse.

"Probably just a raccoon," she said.

"Probably," Michael agreed.

He didn't look as though he believed that any more than she did. Someone had been lurking in the shadows, possibly listening to discover just exactly how much they knew.

CHAPTER
SEVEN

Years ago, when she was still single and living alone, Molly had endured a series of harassing phone calls. They began benignly enough, just like the calls she'd been receiving the last couple of days. But the hang-ups escalated into obscenities, and eventually the nature and frequency of the calls went from the realm of nuisances into very real threats. The caller turned out to be a stranger, a man who'd stumbled on her number by accident and liked the sound of her voice. Even so, she was left with an odd sense of being watched. More than once, she had caught herself looking back over her shoulder, filled with a vague sense of unease.

Since the first hang-up call she'd received after the murder, all of those old nervous feelings had resurfaced, leaving her thoroughly jittery at the sound of the phone. The incident in the shadowy garage tonight didn't help a bit. She left the light on when she went to sleep.

When the phone rang at one A.M., she sat bolt up-right in bed. Instantly wide awake, she grabbed the phone and waited, saying nothing herself. She hung up, only to have it ring again at once. This time she said, "Hello." She wasn't surprised when no one re-sponded to her greeting. Remembering everything she'd been told before about not challenging the caller, about not feeding the desire for a reaction, she quietly hung up. She did make a note of the time, and then she tried to go back to sleep.

The next call came an hour later. Again no one spoke. Again she hung up, but she was losing her pa-tience and her anxiety was mounting. When the fourth call came, though she was quaking inside, she said qui-etly, "I'm recording these calls for the police. I'd sug-gest you stop making them."

"You bitch!" The voice was a low, menacing growl. She couldn't even make out whether it was a man or a woman. She considered trying to goad the caller into saying something more, but the line clicked dead.

Her death grip on the phone had tensed the mus-cles across her shoulders. Anxiety sent perspiration trailing down her back. Every nerve on edge now, Molly pulled the pillows into a stack behind her, turned the radio on to the soothing sounds of WLYF, and sat up, waiting. As the minutes ticked by and then the hours, she realized there would be no more calls, not tonight. At dawn she finally fell into a fitful sleep.

It was less than twenty minutes later when she was jarred awake again. Before she could grab the phone, the ringing stopped. She heard the faint murmur of a voice in the living room, then a crash as the phone clattered to the floor.

"Mom!" Brian yelled, barreling through the door and throwing himself onto the bed, his expression panicky.

His whole body shook as she clutched him to her and tried to soothe him. "Sssh. It's okay. What happened? Who was on the phone?"

"I don't know," he said and again his body shuddered in her arms.

"Did he say something?"

"He said . . . he said you'd wind up like Mr. Winecroft, if you didn't stay away from the cops." His arms clung even more tightly around her neck and his lower lip quivered. "Mom, I don't like this. I'm scared. Maybe we should move. It wouldn't be so bad changing schools again."

Molly could barely control her own trembling, but now hers was less fear than gut-deep fury. How dare someone terrorize her son like this! Instinctively, she thought of Michael. She picked up the card he'd given her, reached for the phone, and dialed his home number.

A soft, musical, feminine voice answered, the accent distinctly Hispanic. So the detective was *involved*. It shouldn't matter, but to her surprise it did. She didn't like the shaft of pure jealousy that shot through her as she waited for him to take the call.

"What is it?" he said seconds later, about the time it would take to pass the phone across a bed. There was no sleepy sensuality to his tone. It was fully alert and all business.

"I think you'd better get over here," she said. Her voice tripped in mid-sentence, then caught on a sob.

"Calm down," he said quietly, using the same soothing tone she'd used with Brian only moments earlier. "What's happened?"

She swallowed hard. "I'll explain when you get here. I think it might be a good idea if you put a tap on my phone, while you're at it."

After that he didn't ask questions. "I'll take care of it. You just sit tight."

Molly managed a faint smile as she ran her fingers through her son's hair. "I wouldn't budge out of this apartment right now if you paid me," she said.

She did, however, persuade Brian to take a bath so that she could shower, untangle her shoulder-length hair, and change. She had too much pride to compete, even just mentally, with that sultry-voiced woman while wearing a faded one-size-fits-all T-shirt with a tiger on the front.

As soon as she'd dressed, she put on a pot of coffee and sat on the sofa to wait, Brian right beside her. They talked about everything except the call that had scared him so.

Michael arrived in far less time than she would have anticipated. It was the first time she'd seen him in anything other than his impeccably tailored suits. He'd obviously grabbed the first thing at hand, jeans and a dress shirt with the sleeves rolled up. He'd combed his hair with his fingers, a sure sign of his rush and his nervousness. Worried lines furrowed his brow. There was an ashen hue beneath his olive complexion and dark stubble lined his jaw. Under other circumstances, she might have indulged in several fantasies about the sexy masculinity of his slightly disheveled look.

The scrutiny he subjected both of them to was thorough. He sat opposite them, legs spread, elbows on knees as he leaned forward to study them intently.

"Are you okay? What the hell happened?"

Molly's response was succinct. "There were more calls during the night."

"How many?"

"Five."

"Hang-ups?"

"At first."

"At first? Why didn't you call right away?"

"I thought he'd give up."

He bit back a lecture, but not a low, heartfelt curse. "But he didn't, right? What happened next?"

"I said I was recording the calls for the police and the caller got nasty."

"You said the caller. Male? Female?"

"I couldn't tell. Maybe Brian could."

"Jesus, you let him answer the phone?" he muttered accusingly. "What were you thinking of?"

"I was asleep," she said defensively. "He got to it before I could pick up."

His gaze shifted to Brian and his tone immediately became gentler, more soothing. "Okay, so you took one of the calls?"

Brian nodded, still clinging to Molly's hand. "Like Mom said, she was still asleep."

"What did the caller say?"

"That Mom would end up like Mr. Winecroft, if she didn't stay away from the cops."

Michael held out his hand and Brian moved to

him. "That must have been pretty scary. I know you'd probably rather not think about it, but could you try real hard to remember if it sounded like a man's voice or a woman's?"

Brian bit his lower lip the way he always did when he was really concentrating on something. "It was real soft, like a whisper, but I think it was a man."

"Had you ever heard the voice before?"

Brian shook his head with certainty. "Never. You won't let anything happen to Mom, will you?"

"Absolutely not, I promise. Now, how about giving your mom and me a couple of minutes alone?"

Brian looked at her uncertainly. Molly said, "It's okay, Brian. Go on and fix yourself some cereal and a glass of juice. It'll be time to leave for school soon."

Alarmed blue eyes met hers. "I can't go to school, Mom. Who'll protect you?"

"I will," Michael reassured him. "I think going to school is a very good idea. I'll drive you over myself."

Brian looked torn. "Do you have a police car with a siren and everything?"

"Nope. Sorry. Just a Jeep. I do have a siren, but it's only for emergencies."

"Maybe this is an emergency," Brian said hopefully.

Michael considered the suggestion seriously. "Maybe it does qualify at that," he said. "Now get moving, so we won't be late."

"Are you sure it's okay to send him to school?" Molly asked as soon as Brian had left the room.

"That's the best place for him. I'll speak with his teacher and the principal, just so they're on the lookout in case anyone hangs around the building who shouldn't be there. The thing to remember is that the caller threatened you, not him. Exactly how much snooping around did you do on your own yesterday? More than I know about?".

"None after you left." At his skeptical expression, she said, "I swear it."

"Then let this serve as a warning. You've already made somebody very nervous. No more conversations with the neighbors, no more secret trips to the scene of the crime."

She shot a startled gaze at him. She'd only walked by to see if the crime scene tape had been removed. It hadn't been. "How did you know about that?"

"They pay me for my astute observations."

"You weren't anywhere near here."

He shrugged. "Astute observation. Lucky guess. In my business they pretty much add up to the same thing. Remember, sweetheart, I have years of experience at this. You have none. It's no contest. I'll out-guess you every time."

"Dammit, we're not playing guessing games. The killer is threatening me."

"Because you're an easy target. Let me be the target. It's what I get paid for." He leaned forward, his gaze intent. "Please, Molly, let it alone. If not for me, then do it for your son. I know what it's like to be a scared kid, to be terrified that you'll never see your mother again."

She heard the surprisingly ragged emotion in his voice and knew that he was telling her the truth. Maybe she just needed to keep him talking. Maybe she needed to understand him, needed to understand this pull that had been there between them despite all the superficial differences and whatever his current involvement was with the woman on the phone. Mostly she needed to trust him.

"How do you know something like that?" she asked. "Did something happen to your mother?"

"Not exactly."

For a minute she thought he wasn't going to say anything more. Something about the memories hurt him deeply. She could see the pain in the depths of his eyes, the hint of vulnerability that after all these years hadn't gone away.

"Thirty years ago I was just a kid in Cuba," he began slowly, his voice quiet. "I lived with my mother and her family. We had no idea where my father was. He was an American GI stationed at Guantánamo. My mother wasn't even sure of his name. She just remembered it was something Irish, so I wound up being Michael O'Hara, instead of Miguel Javier."

Suddenly Molly understood why there were so many incongruities in his personality. The flawless Spanish and unaccented English. The swaggering Latin persona, modified by an intriguing sensitivity. Though he'd never known his father, still he was caught between the cultures.

"I don't remember much about that time," he said, a haunted, faraway expression in his eyes, "except that I was part of a big family and that I was loved. Then one day in 1962 my mother took me to the airport and put me on a plane for Miami. You've probably read about those flights, Operation Pedro Pan, organized by the Catholic Church in Miami and two people inside Cuba. Families packed up their kids and sent them away to save them from Castro, to give them a better life. Some of us were sent to relatives we'd never even met. Some went to live with strangers. Fourteen thousand in all, mostly young boys. I was barely five.''

Molly tried to imagine what it would have been like for a small boy to be separated from everyone he knew and loved. It was impossible. She had grown up with a warm and loving family of her own. Though she sometimes felt her parents' emphasis on high society had been misguided, she'd never known the kind of loneliness or fear that Michael was describing.

''It was three years before I saw my mother again, before she was able to leave Cuba on one of the freedom flights,'' Michael said. ''For most of those three endless years I hated her for what she'd done. I was scared and lonely, even though *Tía* Pilar was good to me. It wasn't until the day my mother arrived in Miami, until I saw how she had been aged by the pain of letting me go, that I realized she had done it because she loved me. You see, for the longest time I thought she'd sent me away just to be rid of me, because she didn't want me anymore.''

There was a telltale sheen in the brown eyes that clashed with hers. ''Don't ever intentionally do anything that could separate you from Brian. Okay?''

Molly couldn't seem to swallow past the lump in her throat. She simply nodded. ''I'll do whatever you say,'' she said finally.

''Go to work. Follow your normal routine. Avoid discussing the murder with anyone. Most of all, don't speculate about what might have happened. Do you have a friend you two could stay with for a few days?"

"Yes, but I'd rather not. It hasn't been that long since the divorce. The move out of our house shook Brian's life up enough. I don't want to disrupt things for him again unless it's absolutely necessary."

"Where's his father? Could he stay with him for a few days?"

"Not a good idea," she said tersely.

"But feasible?"

"Things would have to be a lot worse than they are right now for me to turn Brian over to my ex-husband."

"Is there a problem there?"

"Not really. He's just looking for an excuse to say I'm an unfit mother. He has this idea that a boy should be raised by his father so he won't turn out to be a sissy. Real macho stuff. I mean, maybe he does have a point about a boy needing a male influence. I'm not denying him visitation rights. I'm going to make sure Brian gets involved in Scouts and Little League and all that sort of thing."

"Maybe Brian would like to play soccer," Michael suggested. "I coach a team. Should I ask him?"

As soon as the impulsive words were out of his mouth, he looked as though he wanted to take them back. For her own part, Molly considered the wisdom of allowing her life to become any more entangled with Michael's. Then she thought of Brian and how thrilled he would be to be asked to play on a team. Whatever second thoughts either of them had, her son's happiness had to come first.

"I think it's a wonderful idea," she said.

He nodded briskly. "I'll take care of it, then. The boys seem to have a good time. A lot of them don't have fathers around. I know what that's like. This gives me a way to pay back a little of what I've been given."

"Given?" she said. "It sounds to me as though you've earned whatever you have."

"I'm living in this country. That was my mother's gift. Knowing what I do now about life in Cuba, how could I not be grateful? I'll talk to Brian and see how he feels about it."

Now that Molly had approved, it was between him and Brian. That was what he was telling her. It had nothing to do with her. Okay, she got the message. She could be as generous and understanding as any mother when it came to her son. If Michael asked her to bake cookies for the team, though, she was going to cram them down his throat.

"Do you still live with your family?" she asked, thinking again of that sweet, musical voice on the phone.

"No," he said tersely, his face closed again. Despite the morning's revelations, he was shutting her out, distancing himself from any hint that what was growing between the two of them might be personal. Though she could tell he knew exactly what she was asking, there would be no elaboration, no explanation. She supposed he didn't owe her one, but a little clarification would have set the record straight once and for all.

Then again, maybe she didn't want to know. Things between them were complicated enough. Michael O'Hara's secrets were none of her business.

Naturally, however, the fact that he had secrets at all made her more curious about him than ever. Perversity, thy name is woman! Whoever'd said that had summed up her life fairly accurately.

CHAPTER
EIGHT

Molly did her best to forget all about Michael and the murder. She didn't succeed worth a damn in either case. As a result her temper was frayed. When a producer called at midmorning with some petty annoyance about a location for his TV movie, she uncharacteristically bit his head off.

"I have a murder of my own to worry about. I don't have time to deal with yours. Leave the body in the Everglades for all I care."

Vince overheard her and grabbed his own extension. "Sorry, Greg. Molly's under a lot of stress just now. Let me help. What do you need?"

She knew she ought to be grateful. Instead, she was merely irritated that Vince, of all people, was suddenly the voice of reason in the office. When he'd soothed Greg's ruffled feathers, he hung up and stepped into her office. He lingered near the door, probably so he could flee if things got too tense.

"You okay?" he inquired cautiously.

"No. I feel so darned helpless. I ought to be doing something, but Michael . . ."

His brows rose suggestively. "Michael, is it?"

"Get your mind out of the gutter, Vince."

"Hey, I saw the way the man looked at you the other day. What's the story? Is he single? Go for it, Molly. You're not getting any younger."

She groaned. "Twenty-nine is hardly ancient and I don't need you as my social life guru."

"Who better to give you advice than a man-about-town such as myself?"

"Vince, the kind of relationships you have I'm better off without. Has the word commitment ever crossed your lips?"

"Heaven forbid," he said, looking horrified. "That doesn't mean it's not okay for some people. Boring people. Dead people."

Despite herself, Molly smiled, albeit weakly. "You're incorrigible."

"But cute, right? Now about your cop, you have to send him the right signals." He began to warm to his subject. "I mean, it does get a little complicated since he's investigating this murder and all, but once that's wrapped up, it should be clear sailing."

"He has a live-in girl friend."

"That could be tricky," he said as if it were no more than a minor inconvenience. "Are you sure? Did he tell you that?"

"No, as a matter of fact, he didn't. I called at dawn. Never mind why," she said, when Vince started to interrupt. "She answered."

"Could have been a housekeeper. Could have been a one-night stand. Did you ask?"

"More or less."

"And?"

"In essence, he said to mind my own business."

"In essence," he mimicked. "What does that mean? You women are all alike. You get bent out of shape over something instead of just asking straight out. You gotta clarify things. The look I saw in that man's eyes the other day was not the look of a man who is committed elsewhere."

"So his attention wanders. Do I need that in my life? No." She said it adamantly, but she wondered. Did she really want anything more than a casual flirtation? Not really. However, there was no need for Vince to know that. It might give *him* ideas.

"But . . ." he said.

"No *but*'s. Attraction isn't love. Chemistry isn't commitment. And I'd like to drop this matter now. Go play golf or something."

Vince sighed heavily, his expression one of disappointment. "Think it over, Molly. You want the advice of an expert, all you have to do is ask."

That afternoon after going home early again Molly couldn't shake Vince's observation about Michael's interest in her. She kept telling herself he'd been mistaken, that Michael had made it clear he would open his heart to her son, but not to her. Even so, with Brian in his room doing homework she had plenty of time to stew over the ambiguities. Wasted effort, she knew. She'd be better off trying to figure out the killer. She found her list and added a few notes. There wasn't much.

She was still at the dining room table an hour later, lingering over a second cup of coffee, her tuna salad untouched. She was going over the list of suspects for the fourth time, when the front door burst open. Before Molly could panic, Liza Hastings breezed in, key in hand, an indignant expression on her face and her red hair standing up in a trendy flattop that had been moussed into place. Fortunately she had the perfect gamine face to carry off the style and the friendly, fearless personality to carry off barging in unannounced.

"Why didn't you wake me?" she demanded, flopping into the chair across from Molly and putting her bare feet onto the seat of another chair. Her toenails today had been painted a deep bloodred, perhaps in honor of the murder. Liza tended toward dramatic statements.

"I didn't even know you were back in town," Molly said. "The last I knew you were on a mountaintop in Tibet."

"That was last month. I've been in Brazil since then. I wanted to see the rain forest before it all vanished. I got back late yesterday afternoon. I've been asleep ever since."

"I'm not surprised," Molly said. Just the recounting of Liza's frequent adventures exhausted her, even as they fascinated her. In another life, devoid of parental expectations and coming-out parties, she would have enjoyed such an impetuous, daring existence. "I'm glad you're back. I really need your advice."

"Not until you tell me everything that happened Tuesday night, and I do mean everything. I ran into

Rhea Wilson downstairs. She said Allan Winecroft was stabbed to death and that you're a prime witness."

As Liza listened, she grabbed Molly's untouched mound of tuna salad and wolfed it down. Her expression reflected her increasing astonishment as Molly concluded, "Which makes me a possible suspect."

"You can't be serious," Liza said finally. "It's ridiculous. Anyone who knows you knows you're incapable of murder."

"Detective O'Hara doesn't know me. Besides, he doesn't seriously consider me a suspect even though my fingerprints are all over the weapon. At least, he says he doesn't. I'm sure he's just trying to keep an open mind. I guess if you're a policeman you can't afford to dismiss anyone too early in an investigation."

"He's wasting his time on you," Liza declared loyally. "But you do have a point. If no one else turns up, it would be just like them to take the easy way out and arrest you. I guess we'd better come up with an alternative. Tell me again exactly who was there for the bridge game?"

"Here, I've made a list." She shoved the paper across the table, grateful to have an ally. "Allan and Drucilla. They played against Roy Meeks and me. Tyler Jenkins and his wife played the Davisons. I didn't know the two couples at the third table. I think one of the women owns a boutique in the Square, the one with all the Italian designs that can only be worn if you're under twenty-five and weigh less than a hundred pounds. Just looking in the window depresses me."

"How do you know she owns it, if you've never been inside?"

"I heard somebody asking her about the shop at

the pool one day. You must know who I mean. You bought that denim outfit in that store.''

"Three fourths of my clothes are denim. It travels well. Weighs a ton, though. Maybe I should switch to linen. That would be the environmentally correct thing to do, wouldn't it?''

Molly was undaunted by Liza's conversational diversions. Eventually she always came back to the topic at hand. "I'm afraid I'm not up on environmentally correct attire," Molly said. "I just know you have to iron linen.''

Liza wrinkled her nose. "That is a problem. So, which outfit?''

"The one with the skirt the size of a postage stamp. How do you have the nerve to wear that out in public?'' Molly wondered, then decided that digression must be catching.

"It doesn't take nerve. It takes dieting.''

Molly glanced pointedly at the scattered crumbs on a now empty plate.

"There are no calories in tuna fish. Every dieter knows that.'' Liza plucked up a wayward bit of celery and popped it into her mouth. "Okay, now, let's get serious. We'll never figure out the murderer, if we don't concentrate.''

"I'm supposed to stay out of it,'' Molly reported dutifully.

"Who says?''

"The police.''

Liza was unimpressed. "Well, you can't just sit back and let them send you to jail, can you? Besides, we're just having a private conversation. It's not as if we're out knocking on doors or something.''

"I suppose," Molly said, doubting that Michael would see it that way. Of course, it was a private conversation. He'd never even have to know. If she picked up any tips from Liza, she could dutifully pass them along.

"Okay," she said, suddenly more cheerful, "what do you know about Roy Meeks?"

"Isn't he the one who walks the beach every morning at precisely seven fifteen, rain or shine, no matter what the tide is? Compulsive, if you ask me. Write that down. It could be important. How did you get roped into playing with him anyway? He's too old for you."

"It was hardly a date. Claire Bates came down with the flu the morning of the game. She called me at work and asked me to take her place."

"How did she pick you?"

"I ran into her at the mailboxes the other night. She mentioned the bridge games. I said I'd played in college, not well, but endlessly. I guess she remembered."

"But there must be others who usually substitute. Did she try them first?"

"I don't know. What's your point?"

"Maybe she wanted you to be there to take the rap."

"Oh, for heaven's sakes, Claire Bates is a sixty-four-year-old widow who sings in the church choir. Does that sound like someone who'd stab a man in cold blood and pin the rap on someone she barely knows?"

"You make her sound like some dowdy frump without a brain in her head. May I remind you that she's head of some high-tech personnel search firm.

She spends at least two hours every morning down-stairs in the workout room and four weeks every year at an exorbitantly expensive California health spa. She's gorgeous enough to appear on the cover of *Lear's,* and she could probably run circles around the two of us."

"Maybe me. Not you. You climb mountains. I don't even use the steps."

"You're missing the point again. What makes you think she didn't have the hots for Allan?"

"Liza!"

"Don't look at me like that. Face it, most things do come down to sex. They don't refer to it as the war between the sexes without good reason. When couples aren't in bed, they're usually battling."

"Let's leave Claire Bates and your twisted philoso-phy about relationships out of this for the moment and concentrate on the people who were playing bridge the other night. You must know more about Roy Meeks than I do. He seemed like a pleasant enough man. He never once looked as though he wanted to throttle the Winecrofts, despite their non-stop bickering."

"If he's the one I'm thinking of, he's a retired psychiatrist."

"That's what Mr. Kingsley said."

"I knew it," Liza said triumphantly. "Freudian, I'll bet. Don't you think he looks the type?"

"Because he has a beard?"

"No. It's those dingy sweaters. I can just see him in some dark, musty room listening to people's secrets. He's probably one of those psychiatrists who attribute all emotional problems to deep-seated hatred of the mother or to premature separation from a pacifier. Listening to the Winecrofts probably made him feel nostalgic."

"What about the Davisons? Do you know them?"

Liza's expression brightened. "Sure. He teaches political science at the University of Miami. She teaches creative writing at Miami–Dade Community College. He's the real academician. Publish or perish and all that. She just wants to get kids excited about writing. They've been married for thirty years. They had a house in Coral Gables in the early seventies. When the kids went away to college, they moved here. They're depressingly normal. No skeletons in the closet that I've ever heard of. Nobody even complains about their grandkids when they come to visit. Actually, for kids, they're pretty cute."

"Capable of murder, either of them?"

Liza shook her head slowly. "I can't picture it."

"Do all these couples socialize outside the bridge games?"

"Dinners occasionally. I think I saw them lined up by the pool one day. Tyler and Allan play . . . *played* . . . tennis together. They might have been doubles partners, in fact."

"Any rifts you've ever heard about?"

"None. Couldn't you tell that night if everyone got along okay?"

"After the initial greetings, the only people who spoke above a whisper were the Winecrofts. These people take their bridge very seriously. They can't wait to turn the results in to *The Islander* for publication. Maybe the mood changes once the final hand is played, but I didn't stick around that long. All that bickering made me uncomfortable. I couldn't wait to escape."

"Which brings us back to Drucilla. Why aren't the police concentrating on her? Isn't the soon-to-be-wealthy widow always the most likely suspect?"

"I know she hates losing, but blowing a bridge game is hardly grounds for homicide. Besides, she says she went home right after I did. Allan was alive when she left."

"She says," Liza mocked. "And you believed her? As for a motive, how about divorce?"

"She wouldn't divorce him over his lousy bridge bid either."

Liza scowled at her. "No, forget the bridge game," she said impatiently. "Molly, you really need to spend more time at the pool. That's where you really find out what's going on around here."

"When would you suggest? By the time I get home from work, the only people out there are as exhausted from working all day as I am. The only thing they're interested in is cooling off. They swim. They leave. They don't hang around to gossip."

"Don't say it like that," Liza said, scowling.

"Like what?"

"That judgmental tone. I'm not a gossip. I can't help it if sound carries out there and I'm naturally curious about human nature."

"Fine. We won't get into a discussion of the ethics of eavesdropping or the admissibility of hearsay evidence. If you know something relevant, just spit it out."

"Okay, don't get testy." Liza paused dramatically. "Picture this. Allan Winecroft was about to divorce his lovely wife of thirty-five years for Ingrid Nielsen, the beautiful bimbette in eight-twenty-six."

Molly stared at her, sure her mouth must be hanging open. "That's just two doors down the hall."

"I know. Tacky, huh? Installing his mistress right under his wife's nose takes a certain amount of nerve."

"Are you sure about this? Surely even Allan had better taste than that."

"Check the deed on the apartment. The buyer's name was printed in the paper, when the apartment was sold two years ago. I saw it myself: Allan Winecroft. I don't know if he bought it as an investment or for Ingrid, but she's in there now."

"Maybe he was just renting to her."

Liza rolled her eyes. "Molly, you are so middle-class."

"Well, she could be renting," Molly said defensively.

"Right. And he was over there at midnight fixing the plumbing."

"How do you know he was over there at midnight?"

"The Loefflers, the couple across the hall, told me. I saw him myself, after that. I wangled an invitation to their apartment for dinner."

"You spied on him?"

Liza shot her a look of disgust. "I did not spy. I spent the evening with a perfectly lovely couple. Mr. Loeffler told me all about dry cleaning."

"Dry cleaning?"

"He owned a whole chain of dry cleaners in Ohio before they sold out and moved here. He even told me how to get that raspberry stain out of my cream silk blouse. It was fascinating.''

"I'm sure," Molly said. "But not nearly as fascinating as the comings and goings in the hall, I'm sure.''

Liza just grinned, refusing to be insulted.

Molly ignored her smug demeanor. Refusing even to consider what Michael would have to say, she picked up the dishes, carried them into the kitchen, and headed for the door. When Liza didn't follow, she said, "Don't just sit there. Let's go.''

"Where?" Liza said, but she was already on her feet, ready for action.

"You don't think I'm going to see Ingrid Nielsen by myself, do you? The police would never forgive me if I got myself murdered.''

CHAPTER
NINE

Molly had been around enough movie sets to understand the charisma of power. Producers and directors exuded it, though some of them had to work harder than others to accomplish it. Even so, she couldn't quite imagine Ingrid Nielsen with Allan Winecroft. Not even in the same room, much less in the same bed.

Talk about odd couples. She was tall. He was short. She was young. He had been heading into his golden years at a downhill clip. She was a statuesque beauty of Miss Universe caliber. He, to put it politely, probably hadn't seen the inside of a gym since high school required him to be there. Tennis had done nothing to reduce his flabby stomach. She spent her days languishing at the pool, fascinated with the latest tabloids. He spent his engaged in high finance. The only possible ground for mutual attraction was money. She wanted it. He had it.

Unless he had to fork it all out to an irate ex-wife.

"Okay, assuming for a minute that you're right about an impending divorce," Molly said thoughtfully as she and Liza waited to take the elevator to the eighth floor. "If Drucilla was about to take her husband to the cleaners, wouldn't she be more likely to wind up with a knife in her back? Both Allan and Ingrid would have pretty powerful motives for knocking her off."

"Your divorce really must have gone more smoothly than most," Liza countered. "Drucilla couldn't afford to take the risk of a nasty divorce. The way I figure it, she probably had some skeleton hidden in the closet. By the time Allan Winecroft finished airing the family scandals, whatever they were, Drucilla would have been publicly humiliated. Worse, she would have lost access to his—by all reports—very deep pockets. With him dead, she gets it all and keeps her pure reputation. She'll be married again by the end of the year, probably to some enterprising businessman half her age."

Molly recalled Michael O'Hara's assumption that Drucilla had been awaiting the arrival of a lover when they arrived to question her. Could that have been the skeleton Drucilla would have killed to hide? "Was she having an affair?" she asked Liza as they took the elevator up.

"If I knew that, so would everyone else. Then there wouldn't have been much risk involved in exposure, would there? If she is, unlike Allan, she is very discreet. There's never been so much as a whisper of scandal that could be substantiated."

"Then what makes you think Allan had any ammunition to take into court, especially if he was having an affair himself? Sounds awfully messy on both sides to me. Or maybe if there was no whispering, it's because there was no scandal. Drucilla's alimony would have been safe enough.''

"No. More likely the old double standard. If he could prove she'd been playing around, his own tawdry little affair would be viewed sympathetically. Male privilege or something."

"So, who should we see first? I thought Ingrid, but maybe we should go straight to Drucilla instead."

"You've already seen Drucilla. She's probably surrounded by her friends now or under sedation or something. I doubt if anyone's in there weeping with Ingrid. She could probably use a sympathetic ear."

As the elevator doors slid open, Detective O'Hara started to step inside. He took one look at Molly, who'd gotten out without thinking. If she'd been smart, she'd have stayed right where she was and gone to some other floor. Any other floor. He gave her one of his *I-don't-believe-this* looks and let the elevator leave without him.

"Explain," he said succinctly as her only route of escape vanished.

Since Molly knew he wouldn't like the explanation, she introduced Liza instead. It was an ideal diversionary tactic. His eyes lit up with an interest Molly found herself envying. She knew better than to think it had anything to do with the murder. Liza always had that mesmerizing effect on men. She radiated the kind of energy that attracted them, though their efforts to evoke a response from her were usually wasted. Liza's trail of broken hearts was legendary, and those were just the ones on the island. She didn't have time for romance, or so she claimed. Molly suspected that her own heart had taken a beating years before and she'd adopted a self-protective shell as a result. Whatever the real story, she'd never shared a word of it with Molly despite their immediate and confiding friendship that began when Molly and Brian moved in across the hall.

The detective's attention wandered only briefly. All too quickly, he focused on Molly again. Under other circumstances, she might have found that satisfying. "Your apartment's on five," he said.

"Yes. And you don't have one. Why are you here?"

"Police business." He glanced at Liza. "And your apartment?"

"Right across the hall from Molly," Liza informed him cheerfully. "Want to drop by and see my collection of African masks? They're quite extraordinary."

"I'll bet they are. Perhaps we should all go take a look." He regarded Molly quizzically. "Unless you had other plans."

"Well, I was going . . ." Her voice trailed off.

"Yes?"

"Never mind. It can wait."

"Actually, we were on our way to visit a friend," Liza said. "Ingrid Nielsen. Do you know her?"

The detective gritted his teeth. "No, but I have the distinct impression I should. Why?"

"Well, for one thing she is absolutely beautiful," Molly said hurriedly before Liza could give them away. She'd only made that promise to Michael hours before. He was not going to be thrilled that she'd forgotten it already.

"And?" he said.

"And what?"

"I'm sure you weren't going to see her because she's beautiful. What's her connection to the case?"

"Who said there was a connection?"

"You did."

"I never . . ."

"Your face gave you away. Unless my detecting skills are rusty, which they rarely have time to get, you're still worried about being considered a suspect despite my reassurances just this morning. That means you're probably ignoring my advice to leave the investigating to me . . . again. Are you following me so far?"

She nodded reluctantly.

"How am I doing?"

"You're on the money," she conceded grumpily.

He beamed. "Swell. Then the only thing left to figure out is what this Ingrid Nielsen has to do with Allan Winecroft's murder. Suppose we all drop in together?" He turned back down the hall. "Which apartment?"

"Oh, what the hell," Liza said, leading the way. "The more the merrier."

Molly wasn't so sure about that. Michael didn't look very merry.

His mood improved considerably when Ingrid Nielsen opened the door, her blond hair pulled back from a face so stunning that any agency in New York would have hired her as a model in an instant. Thick lashes rimmed eyes of navy-blue velvet. She was wearing an oversized hot-pink T-shirt that barely reached her knees and clung to every lush curve of her young, tanned body. What he couldn't seem to pull his gaze from, however, were the tears tracking down her cheeks. She swiped at them with a fistful of crumpled Kleenex.

Liza didn't waste time being coy. She drew the girl into a hug. "I'm sorry. You must be feeling absolutely lousy."

Ingrid didn't even spare her a glance. Her frightened eyes were riveted on Michael.

"This is Detective O'Hara," Liza said briskly, ushering them all back into the living room. "He's going to find Allan's killer."

The announcement brought on a fresh onslaught of sobs, all the more devastating because the young girl made not so much as a whimper of sound. Michael stared at her with the bemused expression of a man totally at a loss. Molly almost felt sorry for him, until she realized that his attention had already moved on.

His gaze went to the silver-framed photograph of Allan sitting in the middle of the huge marble coffee table and froze there. She could see the pieces click into place. A fresh arrangement of long-stemmed apricot roses sat beside the photo. The florist's card had been crumpled, then smoothed out. Molly edged closer for a better look. She wasn't surprised to see that the flowers had been sent by Allan. Posthumously, though? Maybe the man had placed a standing order and no one had thought to cancel it. At forty bucks or more a dozen, a greedy florist might be reluctant to cancel the order himself until he was told to.

"Ms. Nielsen," Michael said quietly, "what was your relationship with Allan Winecroft?"

"He was . . ." she began, but her voice choked

up on her. She cleared her throat and looked him straight in the eye. "We were going to be married as soon as he divorced that bitch down the hall."

Molly winced at the blunt description of Drucilla. Michael's face remained stoically impassive. "Did he have any immediate plans to do that?"

"He told me it had to be handled carefully."

Which meant, Molly thought, that Allan had been dragging his heels. Why? She voiced the question aloud.

"Because the old witch controlled all the money."

If the others were as stunned as Molly, they did a better job of hiding it. If all their suppositions about the source of the Winecroft money had been wrong, it played havoc with any motive Drucilla might have had for murder. She could have dumped Allan in a heart-beat. "I thought he had been CEO of a big corporation in New York," Molly said.

"That's true, but it was her company originally. He took it from a nothing little business started by her father and turned it into a conglomerate. He deserved all the credit and she knew it, but she still controlled the purse strings. He told me all about it. If she'd cut him loose, he would have lost everything."

"Then where was he getting the money to pay for this apartment?" Liza blurted, not fearing to rush in where Molly wasn't about to tread.

Ingrid shrugged, obviously not one to question a gift horse. "He had a few things going on the side, I guess. I never asked. Or maybe he took the payments out of petty cash. It's not much of an apartment, com-pared to what they own. I asked him to get a bigger place, but he said he couldn't afford it, all because of

that awful wife of his. I hope you arrest her," she said
to Michael. "She probably killed him just for spite.
She didn't want me to have him."

Molly glanced around at the expensive furnish-
ings, the decorator touches. There had been one brief
moment when they'd first walked in when she had felt
sorry for Ingrid. She'd seemed like a girl who'd innocently gotten caught up in something sordid and was
now paying the price. Now Molly wondered if she
wasn't just a grasping, spoiled brat, perhaps even more
of a manipulator than the woman she sought to replace. It dismayed her how often ugliness turned up
when the veneer of beauty was scraped away.

Having surmised Ingrid's true colors, Molly wondered if Allan had provided for her in his will. If so,
perhaps Ingrid had tired of waiting to share wedded
bliss with him and gone for the payoff. She decided
against asking straight out about the contents of any
will. The girl would only lie. She seemed more than
capable of protecting her own hide.

"What will you do now?" Molly asked, managing
to sound sympathetic.

"Do?"

Getting a job was clearly a concept with which Ingrid wasn't familiar. "Will you be able to stay on
here?" Molly persisted. "Or will you need to go back
to modeling?"

Michael O'Hara shot her an approving glance.

"I'm getting too old to model," Ingrid said, too
quickly. "Besides, I'm sure Allan arranged for me to
keep this place in case anything ever happened to
him."

"Your name was on the deed?"

Ingrid managed to look demure. "He was a very considerate man."

"And very generous," Molly observed. "I'm sure you're right. He must have worried, though, at his age, that something could happen to him and you would be left with nothing. An apartment like this is expensive to maintain. Did you ever talk about that?"

Ingrid's eyes suddenly narrowed. "You mean a will, right? Well, of course he had one. Any man in his position would. We never discussed the contents, though, not specifically."

"So you don't know that he left you anything besides the apartment?"

A fresh batch of tears appeared, as if on cue. "What does any of that matter now?" she whimpered. "All that matters is that he's dead."

By this time, though, Molly doubted if anyone in the room believed the performance, except possibly Ingrid herself.

● ● ●

"Fascinating," Liza said, the minute the door had closed behind them. "Molly, I had no idea you could cross-examine anyone like that."

"Me, either," Michael admitted. It wasn't said with the sort of admiration Molly would have preferred. "Was I wasting my breath this morning? What the hell possessed you to go traipsing up here on your own without telling me what you were up to?"

"You'd have told me to stay out of it."

"Damn right, I would. After last night, you should know better."

Liza stared from one to the other, obviously confused by the crackling tension arcing between them. "What happened last night?"

"It was nothing," Molly murmured.

"Then why did you wake me from a dead sleep to tell me about it?" Michael demanded. "You were practically incoherent."

"I had an attack of nerves, okay? That's all it was. That's hardly incoherent. By the time you got over here I was just fine."

"Fine? I don't think so. Let me remind you one more time that amateur snooping is the fastest way I know to go from witness to victim."

Molly shivered but remained defiant. She wasn't going to allow this whole awful situation to make her run and hide or stop looking out for her own interests. "Look, I got Ingrid to admit that she's probably better off with Allan dead than she was with him alive. That makes her a suspect, right?"

"Yes," he said grudgingly. "But you've also warned her that we're on to her. Any evidence we were likely to get could wind up buried so deep now that we'll never find it."

Liza patted his cheek consolingly. "Don't look so glum, Detective. I'm sure you'll be able to find whatever you put your mind to. Now, come along and tell us what else you've discovered today. I'm sure if we all put our heads together we can have this solved in no time."

"I have lots of help from my fellow officers, thanks."

"Ah, but they don't know the cast of characters the way we do, do they?"

"No," he said, barely controlling a sigh of regret.

"Then come along. Molly makes a great *café cubano*. While she's doing that, we can all get better acquainted."

Molly had a feeling things were spinning out of control. Liza had a way of taking charge that wasn't always appreciated. "I'm not sure getting better acquainted goes along with police procedure," she said, offering the detective an out she was sure he'd grab. He'd obviously seen more of her in the past few days than he'd cared to.

"That's your trouble, Mrs. DeWitt. You don't understand a damn thing about police procedure. I think getting acquainted is definitely in order."

He even led the way to her apartment. When he walked through the door, Brian took one look at him and said, "Oh, wow, you haven't arrested Mom, have you?"

"Not yet," he said with a pointed glance in her direction.

Molly took the hint and practically ran into the kitchen. To her dismay, the detective was only one step behind her. When she toppled the can of Cuban coffee onto the floor, he picked it up and took over. His movements were efficient and practiced. When the powerful coffee was brewing, he turned toward her again.

"Why won't you leave this investigation in my hands?"

"Because I've learned through the years not to count on anyone but myself. There are fewer disappointments that way. If things get screwed up, I have no one to blame but myself."

"In this instance, there is more at risk that way.

Assuming that you're not the killer, which I do assume, by the way, then the real murderer could get very nervous at all your snooping. For all we know, he or she could already think you know too much. We've been over this before. If you insist on pursuing this, the only way I'll be able to protect you is by putting you under guard. Frankly, I don't have the manpower to waste on a meddlesome woman who insists on jumping into the path of danger."

"Thanks," she muttered, thoroughly miffed. *Meddlesome woman,* indeed.

"You know what I mean. You work for the county and know every bit as much as I do about the budget crunch, I'm sure." A wicked gleam put sparks in his dark-brown eyes. He took a step closer. "Unless, of course, you're hoping I'll move in, just to protect you."

"Detective O'Hara," she protested.

"Michael, please," he reminded her, inching closer still. She could smell his after-shave. It was a spicy scent she particularly liked. If he'd meant to intimidate her, it wasn't working. On the contrary, she was likely to throw herself into his arms in another humiliating second.

"It appears we're going to be better acquainted than I ever dreamed," he murmured, deliberately provoking her.

Reacting on cue, Molly gritted her teeth. "I do not want you—or anyone else—to move in here to protect me."

"Actually, it could be convenient," he said thoughtfully, his gaze locked with hers. "It's a long drive from Little Havana. It would save me time if I just bunked on your sofa.''

"I'm sure the county can still afford to pay for your mileage.''

"I was talking time, not money. Just think what clues I could pick up if I lurked about the halls at all hours.''

"And your roommate? What will she think?''

"Bianca does not interfere in my work.''

Naturally, Molly thought sourly. The *little woman* wouldn't. Chauvinist pig. Reminding herself that she absolutely hated his sort of macho superiority helped to slow the pace of her pulse, but not by much.

"Well, I for one think it's the perfect solution,'' Liza said from the doorway, where she'd once again been indulging in her favorite form of entertainment, eavesdropping. "I know that I would feel much safer having you close by.''

"Then invite him to your apartment,'' Molly suggested.

He shook his head. "You're the one more likely to be in danger.''

"Liza is every bit as nosy as I am.''

"But she wasn't around when the murder occurred. You were.'' He nodded decisively. "The more I think about it, the better I like it.''

"Well, I don't.'' She shot Liza a frantic plea for help. Liza was studiously watching the coffee perk and humming.

Michael ignored the objection. "I'll get my things and be back in time for dinner. My treat.''

"This is not orthodox police procedure,'' Molly said desperately. "The director will hate it.''

He winked at her as he headed for the door. "And I've already reminded you that you don't know beans about procedure. Call my boss and complain, if you object. He'll only tell you I'm here for your own protection, which is what I intend to tell him myself."

"Well, who the hell is going to protect me from you?" she demanded before she could stop herself.

Unexpectedly flirtatious brown eyes raked her up and down. "You don't have a thing to worry about on that count," he said insultingly. "You're too skinny. You know us Latin types like our women to have hips. It bodes well for breeding."

"Breeding!" Molly's voice climbed an octave as she repeated the offensive word.

He was chuckling as the door closed behind him. She glared at Liza. "This is all your fault. You had to go and encourage him to stay. I'm sure I could have talked him out of it."

"Why on earth would you want to talk a hunk like that out of staying in your apartment? I don't think your Detective O'Hara is easily swayed once he's made up his mind."

"He is not *my* anything."

"You could do worse."

"Right at the moment, I can't think of how."

"You could wind up with someone like Allan Winecroft."

"Bite your tongue."

Liza grinned. "I wonder where he'll take you to dinner. That Chinese restaurant in the Sonesta's good. Maybe Stefanos for Italian."

"He'll probably bring back a couple of slices from New York Pizza. Why are we talking about this? How am I going to explain him to Brian? It'll scare him to death, if he thinks we're in danger. The calls last night have already made him nervous.''

"Don't worry about Brian. He'll be thrilled to have a cop in the house. It'll give him something to talk about at school."

"I'll be lucky if he doesn't steal his gun to take to show-and-tell. Maybe Brian should stay at your place for a few days."

"Now that really would require some explaining, or do you want him to get the idea that his mother and the detective are having a passionate fling?"

"Brian is too young to know about passionate flings."

"I doubt that, but assuming he is, then he'll probably just feel abandoned and his psyche will be ruined forever. He's better off right here in his own bed . . . unless you would prefer to be alone with the detective," she said slyly. "Are you interested, Molly?"

"Go to hell, Liza."

"No time. I have a date. See you in the morning."

She breezed out, leaving Molly with a whole lot more to fear than the vague possibility that some unknown killer might decide to come after her. The biggest danger to her tonight was going to be having Detective O'Hara in her apartment, within a few skimpy yards of her raging and thoroughly irrational hormones.

CHAPTER
TEN

Brian was watching a crash-bang rerun of *The Dukes of Hazzard* when Molly went to tell him that Detective O'Hara—Michael—was moving in temporarily.

"Okay," he said, barely sparing her a glance. The news clearly didn't faze him. It irritated her no end that Liza, who claimed to have absolutely no maternal instincts, seemed to know her son better than she did. She'd also been hoping that somehow his reaction would provide her with an excuse to keep the detective off her sofa.

"What's for dinner?" Brian asked instead.

Molly sighed, resignation washing over her along with an undeniable spark of anticipation. It was a spark she intended to ignore if she had to spend the entire night under an icy shower. "I don't know. He's taking us out."

"Okay." On the screen two cars playing bumper

tag on some country road crashed into a fiery mess. "Yeah!" Brian said. "Did you see that, Mom?"

Molly cringed. "I saw it. Don't you have homework?"

"Just spelling stuff. I know the words."

"Are you sure?"

"Sure, I'm sure. Spelling's my best subject. You know that." During all of this his eyes never once left the television screen. He was saved from a motherly lecture about driving safely by a timely knock on the door. Since it was too soon for Michael to be back, she checked carefully before answering it. A week ago she wouldn't have bothered, trusting the guards to keep her safe from unwanted visitors.

Claire Bates stood on the threshold, still pale from her bout with the flu but looking every bit as glamorous as Liza had noted in their earlier conversation. Her chin-length hair had been streaked a soft ash blond. She was wearing linen slacks in a pale celadon green with a matching silk blouse and flat shoes just one shade darker. Chunky silver jewelry completed the fashionable ensemble. Her gray eyes were faintly troubled.

"I probably should have called first," she began apologetically.

"No, of course not. Come in. I've just made some Cuban coffee, or I could fix you a cup of tea."

"Nothing, thanks. My stomach's still pitching and rolling like a boat on the high seas. I had to come and see you to apologize for getting you mixed up in this awful business with Allan." She perched on the edge of a chair, her hands folded in her lap, her legs crossed demurely at the ankles. Only a former debutante who'd excelled at hiding her own nervousness would have picked up on the fact that her hands were anything but relaxed.

"Claire, please," Molly protested. "It's certainly not your fault. You could hardly know that Allan would be killed after that card game. You could help me figure out what might have gone on, though. There's a lot I just don't understand."

Alarm seemed to flare in the depths of those silvery eyes. "How could I do that? I wasn't there."

"But you know everyone who was there much better than I do. You could tell me how everyone usually interacts. Maybe then I could tell if anything was particularly off that night."

"Such as?"

"Is everyone in the group friendly?"

The calm facade slipped, replaced by unmistakable fear. "Dear God, you don't think that one of them did it, do you? That's not possible, surely. It had to be a stranger."

Molly shook her head. "I don't think so. I checked the logs that morning. No one came in or out of the building after midnight except residents. I double-checked the log at the gate just to be sure. There's no other access. Even if someone climbed the fence from the beach, the building doors are locked."

Claire shivered and turned paler still. "Maybe it was someone the guard knew well, but not a resident. Sometimes they get a little lax about enforcing the rules, especially with frequent visitors."

"No, this was a new guard. He wouldn't have recognized anyone. He even stopped me three nights ago, because I didn't have the new sticker on my windshield. I'm absolutely convinced that the murderer has to be from this building."

"Oh, God, how awful."

"But you can see why it's so important to think about any rifts, no matter how seemingly insignificant. The Winecrofts were arguing all during the game. Do they usually do that?"

Claire's face reflected her distaste. "I've never known them not to argue. I swear I can't see why she put up with him and that little nobody he installed down the hall. He'd been humiliating her like that for years. Ingrid is new, but she was hardly the first."

"Why on earth didn't Drucilla divorce him then?"

"He kept the business going and maintained all the right social contacts. He smoothed her way onto all the right boards. Besides, in some bizarre way I think it suited her purposes to stay married to a man like Allan. It gave her the freedom to do whatever she wanted to do."

Aha, Molly thought. Now they were getting somewhere. "You mean affairs?"

To her disappointment, Claire shook her head. "Not that I know of, though I've certainly heard the rumors that she was seeing this one or that one on the sly. I was thinking of all the social things she thrives on, the board of this, the luncheon committee for that. If she'd had to run the company herself, she wouldn't have had time left for the things she really enjoys. She likes playing lady bountiful. Drucilla goes to more balls and luncheons than any other five women I know. If she's not being honored herself, she's on the committee to honor someone else. It would drive me crazy. What could they possibly have had left to talk about after six or seven of those things in a row?''

A murder, perhaps? Molly resolved then and there to accept the invitation she'd just received to a benefit luncheon on Tuesday for some disease. She'd planned to send a check anyway, but the cause was suddenly far less important than the conversation. Drucilla had been listed as the event's honorary chairwoman.

"So Drucilla wouldn't be your number one suspect?'' she said to Claire.

"Absolutely not. And Ingrid, for all her lack of morals, would be pretty far down the list too. Allan was her meal ticket.''

"How did they meet?''

"I believe she did a commercial for one of his subsidiaries. It so happened he was meeting with the account executive in New York that day and the guy took him along to the shoot. Apparently it was her last job.''

"If she was a model, she could certainly work down here. Agencies are shooting ads all over town.''

"Allan didn't want her parading that body in front of anyone but him.''

And all the residents of Ocean Manor, Molly thought, but didn't say. "Okay, so she gives up her career for him. What if she suddenly realized he was never going to get a divorce and marry her? Wouldn't that give her a motive?''

"Maybe, but she was probably better off with things just the way they were. She had his money and her freedom, especially during the summer when he and Drucilla went north.''

"He didn't take Ingrid along?''

"Absolutely not. Their circle of friends up there would never have tolerated it. Drucilla comes from old money. They have their standards, even when it comes to affairs. Ingrid lacks class. Her presence would have been an embarrassment to Drucilla and Allan. And for all his flaws, he would never have subjected Ingrid to that sort of ridicule."

"Interesting that he seems more concerned with his girl friend's feelings than his wife's."

Claire shrugged. "I'm sure he felt Drucilla was well able to fend for herself. She may be able to portray the fragile feminine flower to the hilt, but underneath she has a will of iron."

Molly sighed. "If you eliminate Drucilla and Ingrid as suspects, who else is left? Tyler Jenkins? The Davisons? Roy Meeks? Any of the other couples there that night?"

Claire just shrugged helplessly. "I can't imagine any of them being involved. Allan was Tyler's protégé, if it's possible for a sixty-eight-year-old man to have a sixty-two-year-old protégé. At any rate, he was counting on Allan to turn the management of the building around."

"What if he'd been disillusioned? Maybe Allan wasn't tough enough."

"You've got to be kidding. The man was leaving a trail of enemies because of his rules and regulations."

"There," Molly said, suddenly hopeful. "That's exactly what I need. What enemies?"

"Three fourths of the people in the building resented him for treating them like children. Maybe in their hearts, they knew he was after better management, but his whole focus seemed to be on such petty stuff. Getting rid of that cat, for instance. Have you talked to Mrs. Jenko?"

"Yes."

"What about the Firths? You heard about that incident over little Hettie's bare feet? Call them." Claire scribbled a number on a piece of paper. "There are a dozen more like them, who had run-ins with Allan over petty annoyances."

"Maybe some weren't so petty."

"Maybe not," Claire said, still looking every bit as troubled as she had when she arrived. "I guess you always assume a murder is going to be over something big, something important. Not over whether or not some kid was barefooted in the lobby."

"And you're certain there were no deep-rooted feuds among the bridge players themselves?"

"The same people have been playing bridge on Tuesday nights since the building opened. Sure, there have been squabbles. Occasionally somebody gets especially worked up over a hand. Once Tyler accused Roy Meeks of cheating."

"What did Roy do?"

"He quietly folded his hand, stood up and said he'd be back when Tyler apologized. At the time Tyler swore that Roy would get an apology when hell froze over. He held out until the next Tuesday morning, then called Roy up. The game went on as usual Tuesday night."

Neither man's behavior was indicative of the kind of fury it had taken to drive that knife into Allan's back. "That's it?" Molly said.

"I'm sorry. I can't think of anything."

"How did you feel about Allan?"

Claire gazed unflinchingly into Molly's eyes. "I thought he was a nasty, abrasive ass, but I wouldn't have killed him. It takes too long to find a decent bridge player."

"Actually, Allan was pretty lousy the other night."

Claire seemed genuinely surprised by that. "Then his mind must have been on something else," she said with certainty. "He and Drucilla almost never lose."

Perhaps, Molly thought, his mind had been on those late-night threats or on some meeting he had scheduled for after the bridge game. Who was it Drucilla said had stopped by later? Juan Gonzalez? Molly didn't know him, but perhaps she should.

"Do you know anything about Juan Gonzalez?" she asked.

Claire shook her head. "Very little. I think he's a doctor, or maybe it's a lawyer. Anyway, he's very smooth, very polite. A bachelor."

"Were he and Allan friends?"

"I wouldn't think so. I don't recall ever seeing them together. If anything, I would have guessed he and Drucilla were friends."

"More than friends?"

Claire looked startled. "Why, no, I don't think so." She hesitated. "Now that you mention it, though, there was something . . ."

"What?"

"I can't put my finger on it—an intimacy, I guess you'd call it. It was the way they looked at each other when they thought no one was noticing. I never saw them alone, just at parties, occasionally at the pool, always with others around, including Allan. Why would you ask, though? Juan wasn't there that night. He doesn't play bridge as far as I know.''

"Drucilla said he stopped by after I left. She said he'd come to see Allan, that he and several others were sitting around discussing business, when she left.''

"Possible. The men often did that.''

"Thanks, Claire,'' she said, walking her to the door. "You've been a big help. If you think of anything else, let me know.''

"Perhaps she should let *me* know,'' Michael suggested, slowly removing his sunglasses so that Molly could get a good look at the storm brewing in his eyes. He was standing in the hallway, just close enough to have overheard yet more incriminating evidence that Molly hadn't mended her ways. She refused to feel guilty about it, not when she'd learned a couple of interesting tidbits to pass along.

"It's okay,'' she said soothingly, smiling brightly. "I'll share what I know with you.''

"I do so love a witness who's willing to cooperate with the police.''

"Police?'' Claire repeated weakly. "Oh, my.''

Molly practically pushed her into the hall. "We'll talk again soon.''

Claire was only too willing to take the hint. She virtually ran for the elevator.

Michael brought in a small canvas bag and a suit still in its dry cleaner plastic. He hung them neatly in the hall closet without asking directions or permission. Molly edged back into the living room, trying to figure out what she could put between her and the explosion she knew was coming. Since nothing looked suitably sturdy, she decided to rely on her wits.

"She dropped in. I didn't invite her."

"And who is she?"

"Claire Bates, the woman I substituted for on Tuesday night."

"And what did you and Mrs. Bates have to talk about?"

"This and that."

"Care to be more specific?"

"She gave me the Firths' phone number." She waved the paper for him to examine. "They're the people Allan harassed because their child was in the lobby without shoes."

"And?"

"I haven't called them yet."

"I meant, what else did you and Mrs. Bates talk about."

"Actually there is one thing that might interest you. I think I know who Drucilla might be involved with, and he was there Tuesday night."

For one lingering instant fury warred with curiosity. Michael was too good a cop to let the fury interfere with possible evidence. "Spill it."

"Juan Gonzalez."

"Any specifics?"

"Claire's gut instincts. I mean, she didn't think of that at first, but when I asked the question, she thought about it and said yes."

Michael groaned. "Well, that's certainly something we can take into court."

"Okay, so it's not exactly solid," she said, miffed at

his reaction. "It's a lead, isn't it? Shouldn't you be grateful?"

"Oh, I am," he said. "Do you have a spare key for this place?"

Molly blinked and stared. "A key?"

"So I can get back in later."

"You actually want me to give you your own key?"

"Unless you'd rather wait up. Sounds cozy. I'd like that."

"I thought you were taking us to dinner."

"I was, until I got this hot new lead. Now I'm going to spend the evening tracking down Juan Gonzalez and asking him about his current romantic entanglements."

"Not without me you're not. It's my lead."

"It *was* your lead. Now it's mine. I've got the badge that says so. Night, sweetheart. Never mind about the key. I'll just jimmy the lock."

Furious, she grabbed the closest heavy object to throw at his retreating back. Unfortunately, it was her key ring. It struck the target and clattered to the floor. He picked it up, jingled it cheerfully, and tucked it in his pocket. "Thanks. Sleep tight."

The only satisfactory projectile within reach now was a brass lamp with a marble base. It had cost over three hundred dollars. Even so, she had her hands around it when the door shut quietly behind him. She was tempted to sit up half the night if she had to, just for the satisfaction of heaving it at him when he finally came in.

Instead, she found her extra set of keys, told Brian to order a pizza for himself, and called Liza for the apartment number of the couple who'd monitored the comings and goings at Ingrid's apartment. Perhaps they'd seen Juan Gonzalez popping in on Drucilla at odd hours as well.

• • •

Mr. and Mrs. Irv Loeffler were just about to go out for the evening when Molly knocked on their door. Mrs. Loeffler, Tess, was a tiny woman with keen, animated eyes. The minute Molly introduced herself as a friend of Liza's, those eyes sparked with lively curiosity.

"Irv, call the restaurant. Change the reservation."

"We'll miss the early bird special," he grumbled, but he took his plaid jacket off and hung it neatly in the closet. The instincts of a man who'd pressed too many rumpled coats in his day, no doubt.

"So we'll pay full price for a change," Mrs. Loeffler countered. "We can afford it. You cleaned enough suits to pay for dinner out once a week."

Despite his grumblings, Irv Loeffler had a twinkle in his eye when he went to phone the restaurant.

"Now, you come right on in, dear, and tell me why you've come."

Once she was seated, Molly hesitated. It wasn't exactly tactful to suggest that the couple was in the habit of spying on their neighbors. "Actually, it's about the Winecrofts. Did you see them often?"

"Socially? Oh, my, no. Irv and I mostly keep to ourselves. We both like to read. Probably a habit from living in Cleveland. In the winter about the only thing the place was fit for was curling up in front of a fire with a good book. Our children skiied, but not Irv and me. What with one thing and another we were always too busy to learn. Besides, there's nothing I like better than a good mystery."

"Then you must be fascinated with Allan's murder?"

"Actually, that's a little too close to home for my taste," she said nervously. "A good puzzle in a book, that's the ticket."

"Have the police questioned you at all?"

"That nice detective with the Irish name came by, but I told him the same as I'm telling you. Irv and I didn't see the Winecrofts much, except at the elevator occasionally."

"But you knew about Ingrid?"

She shook her head. "Can you believe the nerve of the man? Parading that woman right in front of his wife. If Irv ever did something like that, I'd give him what-for, I can tell you that."

"Did Mrs. Winecroft have much company?"

"You mean men, of course. Well, I can't say for sure, not the way I could with Allan and Ingrid, but it did seem to me that she and that attractive Hispanic man were awfully chummy. My mother always told me that appearances are everything. You just don't have a man who's not your husband dropping by in the middle of the morning. Unless he's just there to fix the sink, it doesn't look proper."

"Do you know who he is?"

"José, maybe. Or Jesús. Is that it, Irv?"

"What's that, dear?"

She waved her hand impatiently. "The man who was always dropping by to see Drucilla. Is his name José?"

"That's gossip, Tess. You know how I feel about that."

"Irv," she said in that quiet, warning way that women for centuries had used to suggest dire consequences.

He heaved a sigh of resignation. "Juan," he said. "Juan Gonzalez. Lives upstairs in the penthouse. If you're going to talk about these things, I don't know why you can't keep the names straight. Now can we go to dinner before we miss the second reservation?"

Molly stood up. "Thank you both so much for taking the time to talk with me. I hope you enjoy your dinner."

Tess followed her into the hall. "Don't mind Irv. He's a regular old grouch whenever he has to pay full price for anything. Comes from living through the Depression, I suppose."

"It never hurts to be cautious when it comes to finances," Molly agreed. "How does he feel about the way these assessments keep going up?"

"Oh, please, don't even mention it. He gets apoplectic. Him and Ralph Keller down on two. To hear them tell it, there won't be a retiree able to afford this place if the board keeps on the way it has been."

"Did he ever talk to Allan about the way he felt?"

"He wrote him a letter, the same one he'd sent to Manny Mendoza the year before. The board doesn't pay a bit of attention to folks like us. They're a regular little clique. I'm surprised Allan was able to budge Manny Mendoza out in that last election. Of course, there's talk all the time that it was fixed."

"What about Mr. Keller? Did he complain?"

"Well," she began conspiratorially. "I wasn't

there, but I hear he and Allan had quite a set-to out at the pool one day. If Irv hadn't grabbed Ralph's arm, he would have pushed Allan straight into the water."

"Did you mention that to Detective O'Hara?"

"Why, no. Oh, my, you don't think that Ralph . . . why, he would never kill anyone. Besides, he couldn't have done it."

"Why not?"

"The way I hear it, Allan was murdered late at night. Ralph is always in bed by ten, same as us."

As alibis went, it wasn't much. Molly decided she'd know more, once she'd had a chance to meet Ralph Keller herself.

"Thanks, again," she told Mrs. Loeffler. "Enjoy your evening."

She practically ran to the elevator and used the phone inside to call the front desk for Ralph Keller's apartment number. The elevator was already on the second floor by the time the guard had found it. She figured she had another ten minutes tops before the pizza arrived.

Outside Ralph Keller's door, she heard the television going full blast. She had to pound to be heard over the news. Finally the door was thrown open revealing a tall, barrel-chested man with a fierce expression.

"I ain't buying nothing," he said and nearly slammed the door. Molly wedged herself into the opening in the nick of time.

"I'm sorry, Mr. Keller. I'm not selling anything." She introduced herself. "I was just visiting with the Loefflers up on eight and they gave me your name. Could we talk for a minute?"

"What about?" His gaze narrowed suspiciously.

"The assessments. Mrs. Loeffler says you've been worried about the way they're going up."

"Damn right I am. There's no excuse for it." He hesitated for a minute, then opened the door wide. "Might as well come on in and have a seat."

"Thank you."

Though it was still daylight outside, the apartment was dark. The drapes had been drawn to block out the light and only a single lamp with maybe a sixty-watt bulb had been lighted. It created a circle of pale illumination that barely spread beyond the end table it was on. The place also reeked of pipe smoke. The cherry scent might have been appealing when fresh. Now it was stale, imbedded in every piece of over-stuffed furniture.

"You must be from up north," she guessed, surveying the heavy fabrics and dark woods.

"Trenton. Lived there for sixty-five years. Would have stayed there till I died, but my wife wanted to move south. She came to Miami one February and never got over it being so warm. Insisted we move the day I retired. Don't you know, she passed away that first year. Never really had a chance to enjoy it."

"I'm sorry," Molly said. "I'm surprised you didn't move back."

"Guess I'd adjusted by then. Didn't seem to be much sense in it."

"If it's not too personal, are you on a pension? Social Security?"

He made a sound that might have been a snort of derision or maybe laughter. "No, ma'am. I did okay with my business up there. Had a restaurant, home-style cooking, baked goods, that sort of thing. Opened a second one about ten years ago. The year I retired I sold out to some guy who started franchising 'em. They're all over Jersey now, a couple in New York and Connecticut. Got a nice payout and I'm still getting a little money in from selling him the name.''

"So the assessments aren't going to really hurt you?"

"Lady, I'm not the sort to pinch a penny till it squeals, but I do believe in getting value for my money. This place is operated with a license to steal. No formal bids. No checks and balances.''

"Doesn't Jack Kingsley have to get approvals from the board?''

That strange, rough hoot rumbled through him again. "You try telling him that. Talking to any of 'em is a waste of breath. If somebody's not getting kick-backs, I'll eat that old fedora hanging there on the hatrack."

"I heard you argued with Allan about all this."

"Tried to tell him plain and simple what was happening. He nodded, all polite like, but nothing changed. The next time we talked, I lost my temper. Probably would have shoved him in the pool, if Irv hadn't been there to stop me." He leaned toward her. "If you're thinking I was mad enough to kill him, you're right. I was."

Molly swallowed hard as the sound rumbled again in his chest. He stared her straight in the eye. "But I didn't."

Oddly enough, as creepy as the apartment was, Molly believed him. Which didn't mean, of course, that she wouldn't mention this conversation to Michael when he came in that night.

   Once in her own apartment again, despite her solemn vow to wait up to divulge what she'd discovered, she fell asleep on the sofa. She woke up in her own bed. How she got there didn't bear thinking about.

CHAPTER
ELEVEN

It was a great day for a funeral, at least if you were of the school that considered stormy skies and gloom to be redundant for an already depressing occasion. The Saturday skies over Miami had been washed clean by a brief predawn shower. A weak Canadian cold front, probably the last of the year, had whisked through, leaving behind bearable temperatures and a comfortable breeze.

Even without the good weather, mourners would probably jam the funeral home. Murder, money, and intrigue always drew. Molly did not plan to be among those at the service. Michael thought it best. Satisfied that she would stay put, he had left not five minutes before Liza arrived to convince her otherwise.

"It's our civic duty to go to the memorial," she said. "Allan was an important man on the island."

"When did you become so public-spirited? You're out of town half the time," Molly reminded her,

weighing her own desire to go against Michael's prob-
able fury if she did. Arguing with Liza made her feel
noble. She had *tried* to reason with her, she could tell
him.

"Which makes it all the more important that we
catch the murderer. I won't rest a minute on my next
trip if I have to worry that he's still loose in the
condo."

"That *we* catch the murderer? That's the job of
the police, as Michael reminds me at least once an
hour."

"And I'm sure they're on top of it. But you have to
admit there are angles they might overlook."

Michael O'Hara did not impress Molly as a man
likely to overlook the least little detail. Look at the way
he'd jumped on that Juan Gonzalez business last
night. Whatever he'd found out, he hadn't deigned to
share it with her. Feeling surly as a result and out of
sorts because she'd missed the moment when Michael
carried her to bed, she'd kept her own news to herself.
As for her turning up at the funeral chapel, he was
bound to be highly suspicious of her attendance at a
memorial service for a man she claimed to have known
only slightly. She tried explaining that to Liza. The
words fell on deaf ears. Before she realized what was
happening, she was in Liza's flashy little red car and
on her way to the funeral. Fortunately, she'd been
wearing black. Coincidence? Absolutely.

Okay, she had to admit to a certain curiosity.
Would Allan Winecroft's lover show up? How would
Drucilla react if she did? What about Juan Gonzalez?
Would he be at the side of the mourning widow?
Which of the Ocean Manor residents would appear?

The bridge club participants? Molly scanned the crowd in search of answers.

Unfortunately, the first person she recognized was the homicide detective, who was making his way toward her at a clip that would have caught a running back at full speed. His expression wasn't exactly welcoming. She retreated instinctively to a safe spot behind Liza. Her neighbor's charms were considerable. She doubted that Michael would miss them.

To her astonishment he barely seemed to notice the dramatically attired redhead, whose only hint of black was a diagonal slash across a pristine white dress. His attention never once wavered from Molly's guilt-ridden face. Maybe he couldn't take the glare from Liza's dress.

"Why are you here?" He kept his sunglasses in place, but Molly could just imagine the flash of anger in his dark eyes.

"To pay my respects," she said. It came out sounding more like a question than a statement. Naturally, he caught the hesitation.

"Try again."

"That's my best shot."

Her refusal to be caught up in an argument over her motives seemed to surprise him. He finally nodded. "I suppose it's pointless to ask you to go home, since we discussed all the reasons earlier."

"Yes," Liza said for her. "We're here to help."

"Help who?"

He fastened his gaze on Liza. Well, to be more precise, he turned in her direction. Who could tell where he was looking the way those damned glasses reflected everything right back at you.

"Well?" he said.

"To help the police, of course. You can't possibly know everyone here."

"And you do?"

Liza scanned the crowd thoughtfully. "Yes, I think I do, as a matter of fact."

Michael blinked at the response. "You're joking."

Molly could have told him that Liza made it her business to know people. She'd been a highly successful public relations executive for a number of years, made a bundle, invested it wisely, then sold her business to gallivant around the globe. Occasionally, she guided tours just for the fun of it. At any rate, her PR instincts and her natural curiosity and friendliness kept her well informed on who was who in island life.

"No joke," Liza confirmed. "I get around." She pointed to a cluster of people standing near the doorway. "Mr. and Mrs. Lansing. He owns the shoe store on Miracle Mile in Coral Gables. You know the one, Molly. Designer shoes at discount prices, probably hot."

"Stolen?" Michael said weakly.

"Either that or knock-offs. He couldn't sell at those prices otherwise."

"And their connection with the deceased?"

"Their wives went to Sarah Lawrence together. They have dinner every Tuesday." She glanced at Molly. "Or is it Thursday?"

"Tuesday's bridge night."

"Right, Thursday then," Liza said. She pointed out half a dozen others, offering similar insights into their personalities, their business holdings, and their relationships with the Winecrofts. After an instant of openmouthed astonishment, Michael took notes.

When she slowed, he glanced up. "How about the man standing by himself under the tree?"

Liza studied him for a minute. "He's one of yours."

"One of mine?"

"A cop."

"What makes you think that?"

"His eyes. He's watching the crowd. Nothing gets past him."

"Fascinating," Michael said.

"She's not that good," Molly grumbled. "She saw the two of you talking not five minutes ago."

Liza laughed, her expression unrepentant. "Well, that helped," she admitted. "So, do we get to stay?"

"Could you manage to keep your mouths shut and your eyes open?"

"A tricky skill," Molly retorted, "but I think we can manage it."

"Not me," Liza said. "I came here to ask questions. I'm leaving for China next week and I absolutely refuse to go off while there's a killer loose."

"Perhaps if I had a little more cooperation and a little less interference, I could wrap this up by next week," Michael said.

"I cooperate," Molly reminded him. "I shared that lead with you right away last night."

"Because I walked in and caught you discussing the murder with that Bates woman."

"What lead?" Liza demanded.

Molly pretended she hadn't heard either one of them. She glared at Michael. "On the other hand, you have shared diddly about what you found out.'' Her bargaining position would no doubt be seriously jeopardized if he found out how many other leads she'd developed last night. Right now he was on the defensive, and she liked it.

"Because you were asleep when I got in and I was in a hurry this morning," he said, his expression grim.

"Why didn't you just wake me?"

"Madre de Dios, woman, I picked you up, carried you to your room, and put the covers over you, and you never so much as blinked. Should I have set an alarm?'' The brief explosion of Spanish was indicative of his irritation. It seemed to be a point of pride with him to restrict himself to using English. When he lost his temper, however, Spanish filled the air. Some of it, she suspected, would not be taught in class. "Okay, you're right," she said soothingly. "I don't even remember you picking me up."

Liza edged closer. "How is that possible?" she whispered. "How could you not know the man took you to bed? God, what a waste!"

"He didn't take me to bed," Molly protested, blushing furiously. She absolutely refused to look at Michael. "Not the way you mean. Let's get inside."

"But I want to hear more. . . ."

"I'm going inside," Molly announced firmly. She didn't wait to see if anyone was coming with her. She wedged herself into an aisle seat in an already packed pew. Even if Liza and Michael followed, they'd have to sit elsewhere. She was in no mood to deal with either of them. When they settled together two rows in front of her, she began to understand the kind of irritation that might lead someone to stab someone in the back.

In her case, though, she wasn't sure which of the two she'd go after first.

After the minister intoned several somber prayers and half a dozen people delivered eloquent eulogies, Molly caught sight of the Ocean Manor accountant who had signed off on last year's budget. When he slipped out the back door, she followed.

"Mr. Rawlings, could I have a word with you?"

Stoop-shouldered from bending over a desk for thirty-five or forty years, Rawlings reminded her of a character from some dreary thirties movie, all black and white and gray. He hesitated at the edge of the lawn, squinting at her through thick glasses. "Do I know you?"

"Molly DeWitt. I live at Ocean Manor."

He jammed his hands into his pockets in a nervous search for his car keys. "Sorry, I'm in a rush. Tax season, you know."

"Could I make an appointment, then?" she suggested. At this rate, it was going to be a lost week again anyway. She'd already planned to go to the luncheon for Drucilla at the Intercontinental. She could squeeze Harley Rawlings in on her way to the luncheon if she couldn't persuade him to talk to her right now or she could see him Monday. Vince was going to be thrilled when she announced her schedule for the week.

The accountant's nervousness increased. His gaze darted this way and that, and he continued sidestepping toward the street, as if he could hardly wait to escape. "Did you want me to do your taxes?" he inquired.

"No, actually, I need your help understanding the

building's budget. I'd be happy to pay you for your time."

"No, no, that isn't necessary. I'd be happy to explain it, but you see I'm no longer involved."

"You're not the accountant for Ocean Manor?"

"No, ma'am. Mr. Winecroft fired me."

"Fired you? Could he do that?"

He blinked several times. "Don't know if he could, but he did."

"When?"

"Last Tuesday, as a matter of fact. The day he was killed."

Before she could ask him another question, he scurried away.

"Well, I'll be," she murmured and tried to imagine the five-feet-six accountant jamming that knife into Allan's back in a fit of rage. The picture wouldn't come clear, but that didn't mean it hadn't happened just that way.

CHAPTER
TWELVE

Molly was still staring after Harley Rawlings when the chapel doors opened and the crowd spilled out. Michael was the first one through the door, his gaze scanning the lawn until he found her. He reached her in five long strides, wrapped a hand around her elbow, and kept on moving. Molly had to take quick little running steps to keep up.

"We need to talk," they said simultaneously.

He stopped so fast, she bumped into him. He tilted his head. "Say that again."

"We need to talk."

He gazed at the sky in apparent disbelief. "Where's the lightning bolt," he muttered.

"You don't have to be sarcastic."

"Sarcastic? I'm flabbergasted. Why the turn-around?"

"Let's just say that a few things have come to my

attention, and I thought I ought to share them with you."

"Praise be," he said, along with something in Spanish she had a hunch would blister her ears if she could translate it. "Let's go grab a cup of coffee at that shop across the street."

"Too crowded. There won't be enough privacy. Besides, I want to wait here a minute to see if everyone showed up."

"Everyone meaning?"

"All the suspects. Juan Gonzalez especially. Was he here? Once we got inside, it was so crowded I couldn't see."

"Yes, but you can scratch him from your list."

"Why? I found out for sure that he's been dropping in on Drucilla at all hours, whenever Allan wasn't around. They have to be involved."

Michael took off those blasted sunglasses and regarded her evenly. "You're sure now? This isn't just more wild speculation?"

"Absolutely not. After you left last night, I went to visit the couple across the hall, the Loefflers. I knew from Liza that they knew all about Ingrid and Allan. It stood to reason that they might have seen someone coming and going from Drucilla's."

"And they had seen Juan Gonzalez?"

"Yep. Often."

"Did they see him the night of the murder?"

Molly blinked. "I don't think so. At least they didn't mention it. Besides, they say they go to bed by ten. Why?"

"Because he claims that after he briefly chatted with Allan in the cardroom that night, he came up to see Drucilla and tell her that Allan had agreed to a divorce.''

Molly stared at him. "A divorce? Drucilla wanted a divorce?''

"So it seems, at least according to Juan.''

"If she wanted one and Allan wanted one to marry Ingrid, where was the need for persuasion?''

"As the story goes, Allan had been reluctant to give up his cut of the family fortune.''

"Do you think Juan used that knife to persuade him?''

"He says it was Drucilla's settlement offer that did the trick. In retrospect, I have to wonder, though he did tell me there were half a dozen witnesses that Allan was alive when he left. I checked, and they all confirmed it.''

"Maybe so, but would he have risked going to see Drucilla if Allan was likely to turn up at any moment?''

"What's the risk if Allan already knew all about them?''

"Which we can't prove or disprove now that he's dead.''

"That is the dilemma,'' Michael confirmed. "The alternative theory is that Juan had his talk with Allan about whatever. Afterward, he hung around outside the cardroom until the others left. Then he went back and stabbed Allan. From there he headed to Drucilla's, knowing there was no chance they'd be interrupted by an irate husband.''

Molly glanced toward the doors of the chapel just in time to see Drucilla exit with Juan at her side, solicitously holding her arm as she made her way to the waiting limo. They made a striking pair, he in his dark suit, she with a black mantilla over her red hair.

"So much for discretion," Molly muttered.

Michael steered her to his car. The Jeep, she noticed, had been washed for the occasion, but it still had a clutter of soccer equipment in the back. "Let's go to the grave site after all," he suggested. "See who else is weeping and wailing."

"Speaking of weeping, did Ingrid show? I didn't see her."

"She's over there by the steps."

Mourning became her. Dressed all in black, she looked glamorous and mysterious. She was standing alone, staring at the hearse bearing Allan's body. Occasionally she touched a handkerchief to her eyes. Molly glanced back as the procession drove off. Ingrid was still standing there, clutching one of the apricot roses Allan always sent.

On the way to the grave site, Molly filled Michael in on her conversations with Ralph Keller and with the fired accountant.

"My, my, for a woman who swore off investigating, you have been busy."

"Admit it. They're good leads."

"Yes," he said grudgingly. "I'll check them out myself this afternoon." He glanced over. "I haven't had a chance to ask before. Any calls last night?"

"None."

"Will you and Brian be okay alone in the apartment tonight?"

"Hot date, Detective?"

"It's Easter weekend. I have some family stuff. I could shake loose if you need me there, though."

"Staying in my apartment was your idea, not mine. I'll be fine."

He was quiet for several minutes. His fingers tapped a nervous beat against the steering wheel. "You and Brian could come along," he said, but without much enthusiasm.

"How would you explain that? Would you tell everyone you're holding us in protective custody?" She couldn't keep an edge out of her voice. Why bother to offer, when he knew what he was suggesting was bound to be awkward? No doubt that macho protective streak was surging again.

Challenged, he clenched his jaw. "There's no one to whom I owe an explanation."

"Oh? Bianca might not see it that way."

His smile was rueful. "Probably not."

Molly figured as long as the subject was finally out in the open, she might as well run with it, see how committed he was to the woman who answered his phone in the middle of the night. "So, what's the story with you two? Does she have some claim or not?"

The rhythm of his fingers against the steering wheel picked up. "Depends on whom you ask, I suppose."

"I'm asking you."

The drumming stopped. He glanced sideways for a beat. "Then the answer is no."

Molly held back a desire to whoop with delight. "She doesn't see it that way?"

"Let's just say I made the mistake of letting her think she had a hold on me. We're working it out."

"At the end of this process, do you expect her to go or stay?"

He studiously kept his eyes on the road. He switched on the radio. His fingers began to tap again, beats ahead of the salsa sounds that filled the car. "That's up to her," he said finally. "As long as she understands there's no future for the two of us."

"Then why not just tell her to go? You're copping out, Detective. Using her. Sounds pretty lousy to me."

"Look," he snapped. "I care about her. She's a good kid. She was there when I needed her. I don't want to see her hurt."

"How far will you go with that?" she asked, irritated by his apparent mastery of self-delusion. "Do you plan to marry her so she won't get her feelings hurt?"

He slammed his palm against the wheel. Apparently it was a thought that had crossed his mind before. He wasn't crazy about the question or about what his answer said about his lifestyle. "No, dammit. What the hell business is this of yours anyway?"

"Just trying to see what makes you tick."

"The same hormones that make any man tick."

"A cliché, then? How disappointing."

He glanced in her direction. Molly's own sarcastic expression reflected back at her in the sunglasses. "I wonder something, Detective. I wonder if you're really as tough and controlled as you want everyone to think you are."

"Believe it," he said tersely.

Molly smiled as a reluctant sigh escaped him.

"You know," he said, "my life was moving along just fine before you jumped in and decided to examine it."

She held up her hands, all innocence. "Hey, I'm

just passing through. Solve this murder and you never have to see me again."

"I can't wait," he muttered.

To her regret, it sounded suspiciously as if he meant it.

● ● ●

No mourners threw themselves on Allan Winecroft's casket at the grave site and confessed. Half the suspects weren't even there. Michael didn't even bother to leave the Jeep. He parked it where he could observe the proceedings, then sat there in stony silence. Molly walked over to the plot of newly turned earth and joined the throng listening to the minister's final prayers for Allan's eternal soul. When the graveside service ended, she murmured her condolences to Drucilla and, after casting a speculative glance at Juan, returned to the Jeep.

The ride home was as tense and subdued as any movie set during the filming of the climactic scene. When they reached Ocean Manor, Michael pulled up in front of the building and cut the engine.

"I'm sorry," he said, as if the words were unfamiliar and faintly troubling.

"For?"

"What I said back there. Sometimes you irritate the hell out of me. I've been telling myself it was professional anger. No cop wants an amateur screwing up an investigation. But . . ."

Molly waited. Finally he turned to face her. The sunglasses came off, revealing that vulnerability that was so appealing, and that he so rarely allowed anyone to get close enough to see. "Now I'm not so sure."

"And you don't like ambiguity."

"No."

She risked her own vulnerabilities. "Can I tell you something, without your making a federal case out of it?"

For an instant, he looked almost nervous. "You aren't going to confess or something, are you?"

She grinned. "Not to the murder. I was just going to say that I'm not all that crazy about ambiguity myself. So if you happen to figure out just what it is you are feeling here, let me know."

His gaze locked with hers. He leaned toward her, then caught himself. Instead, his hand cupped her chin and the pad of his thumb caressed her bottom lip. "I'll do that."

Molly's knees were knocking so hard when she got out of the car, she could barely stand. She plastered a jaunty smile on her face and waved as he drove off to spend what was left of the weekend with another woman. Sometimes life sucked.

By Sunday morning Molly's mood had improved slightly, though not enough to convince her that an Easter egg hunt on the grounds would be terrific fun. Brian had his heart set on it, though. She mustered sufficient enthusiasm to drag on her clothes and go out to the pool where the dozens of children and visiting grandchildren were clustered in their holiday finery.

To her amazement, the first person she saw was Juan Gonzalez, surrounded by a trio of dark-haired girls dressed in frilly pink dresses. They were dancing around excitedly, pleading with him to help them hunt for the eggs. "*Niñas,* that would not be fair," he protested, laughing. "You must find the eggs on your own if you wish to win the prize. Now go and listen to the instructions."

"Tío, we need you," the littlest one said earnestly, turning her dimpled smile on him.

So he was their uncle, Molly thought as she walked over to join him. She grinned. "Looks like you have your hands full."

He lifted his soulful dark eyes to the heavens. "Yes. My niece brought the little ones by, then ran off to church. *Niñas,* this is Señora DeWitt." He pointed to the oldest, a plump child of maybe nine or ten. "This is Elena. That is Margarita. And the baby here is . . ."

"I am not a baby, *Tío.* I am 'cesca."

"Francesca," Juan corrected. "She is three and very precocious."

Molly called to Brian and his friends and introduced them. "Boys, why don't you take the girls with you to hunt the eggs. You'll find that many more, if you all work together."

From the disgusted expression on Brian's face, she had a feeling she would pay later for the suggestion, but he did as she asked. Juan looked relieved.

"Thank you. I was not looking forward to crawling around on my hands and knees at my age. Come, join me in the shade."

Molly followed him to two chairs under a striped umbrella. She took the opportunity to study him more closely, noting the distinguished streaks of gray in his coal-black hair, the expensive gold watch and ring, the silk-blend shirt and tailored slacks. Everything about him shouted understated wealth and classic taste. The sparkle of amused tolerance in his eyes when he'd spoken to his grandnieces seemed an unlikely response for a man who might have committed murder only days before.

"I saw how you watched me yesterday, señora. You know about Drucilla and me," he said, his voice quiet. "From the detective, I presume."

"And others."

He shook his head ruefully. "And we thought we had been so careful."

"Believe me, there were no rumors. I asked some of the most observant gossips about that. It was little things, an observation here, a comment there. They added up."

"I see."

Made bold by the crowd around them, Molly dared to ask, "Did you kill him?"

Laughing brown eyes met hers. "You are very brave."

"Not so brave. There are witnesses everywhere."

"Foolhardy, perhaps."

She shook her head. "I don't think so. I can't deny you had the opportunity, probably even a motive."

"And what would that motive be?"

"You're in love with Drucilla. Allan might have proved troublesome, if you had aspirations to her and her money."

"I wanted Drucilla," he emphasized. "Not her money. I have more than enough of my own. I have businesses in Panama and throughout South America. They are not suffering. I would gladly share it all just for her love. She is a remarkable woman. At my age, after a lifetime of travel and experience, it is possible to recognize such value. I doubt that Allan ever appreciated her as he should have. He was a cold, crass man.''

"You still haven't denied killing him."

He shrugged, a subtle lift of his shoulders. "Would my denial make so very much difference? You will reach your own conclusions, no matter what I say."

"Do you have any theories about who might have stabbed him? Was there an argument in the cardroom when you were there?"

"No. If anything, there was a rather dull discussion of the upcoming baseball season. Allan was a Mets fan, I believe. Others preferred the Yankees. All rather tedious. Allan and I spoke in the corridor, and then I left. I presume he returned to defend his team."

A shadow fell across them just then. Molly looked up as Jack Kingsley pulled up a third chair. "Mind if I join you?" he asked, though he obviously wasn't waiting for the invitation. "God, it's hot out here." The freckles across his brow, where his sandy hair had receded, stood out even more prominently than usual. He blotted his face with a rumpled handkerchief.

"The kids look as though they're enjoying themselves," Molly observed, letting the conversation with Juan about the murder drop. "How long has Ocean Manor held the egg hunt?"

"I started it when I came," he said. "Used to do it at a condo up in Jacksonville when my own kids were small. There was some griping about the noise the first year, but after that everyone pitched in to help. Sometimes I think there are more grandkids here for this than come during the Christmas holidays."

"Are your own children here today?" Molly asked.

"No, they're too old for this. Both boys are in college now. One's studying law at Yale, as a matter of fact. The other one's in premed."

"You and your wife must be very proud of them."

"I'll tell you what I'm most proud of. They've never gotten into drugs. Raising kids these days is a crapshoot, with all that stuff around. You'll see for yourself, Mrs. DeWitt. Once Brian gets to high school, even junior high, you'll have to watch like a hawk to make sure he doesn't get mixed up in the wrong crowd. Hard to tell, too. They don't wear signs around their necks announcing it. In my day, you could pick out the tough kids, the ducktail haircuts and black leather jackets, cigarettes hanging out of their mouths. Today they look just like the kids next door."

Molly suddenly felt chilled, even though the temperature was already a humid eighty-five or higher. Only the reappearance of Brian, with Juan's grandnieces in tow, warmed her. With dirt and grass stains from head to toe, he looked wonderfully normal. Francesca and Margarita were equally disheveled. Only Elena's dress remained spotless, her patent leather shoes shiny, her long dark hair unmussed. She carried a basket filled to overflowing with brightly colored plastic eggs.

"Tío, we won," Francesca announced, twirling until she was breathless.

"And what did you win, *niña?"*

"Candy, of course," Kingsley said, smiling at them benevolently. "What would Easter be without lots of

chocolate bunnies, right, girls? Come along and I'll
see that you get your prizes."

Molly glanced at Brian. "Where are your eggs?"

He kept his eyes on the ground. "I gave them to
Francesca," he mumbled. "She couldn't find any."

Molly exchanged a glance with Juan, whose lips
were twitching with amusement.

"You are truly a gentleman," he said to Brian.

"Yeah, well, it's just a dumb game anyway."

Not so dumb, Molly thought, if it taught him such
a valuable lesson about chivalry.

An interesting concept, chivalry. Juan Gonzalez,
with his dignified, courtly ways, personified it. Would
he have quietly provided Drucilla with an alibi for her
own whereabouts at the time of the murder? In effect,
that's what his own alibi had done. It had excluded
him from suspicion, but it had also taken her out of
the picture as well.

It was something a man deeply in love just might
do.

CHAPTER
THIRTEEN

The phone rang at one-hour intervals throughout the night. Each time Molly could hear breathing on the line, but while that was menacing enough, there were no verbal threats. She successfully resisted the urge to call Michael and ask him to come back, but by morning she was shaken and exhausted. It took every ounce of determination in her to drag herself to the office.

Jeannette took one look and began fussing over her. She poured a cup of strong, black coffee and brought it to Molly's desk. "It looks as if you need this, yes?"

Molly held her head up with effort. "Keep it coming and I might survive." She was too groggy to be sure why she wanted to, unless it was to figure out if Juan Gonzalez was trying to protect Drucilla because he was convinced of her guilt.

"What's on the agenda for the day?" she asked Jeannette.

"Larry Milsap called."

Molly groaned. "Don't tell me. Let me guess. He's lost the permits again."

"No, actually, he wants to stop by to discuss an ad he's doing next month. He was thinking maybe Brian would like to be in it."

Molly's flagging spirits revived ever so slightly. Brian would be thrilled. "What's the product?"

"He didn't say. He'll be here at eleven unless I call to cancel."

"I should be able to stay awake that long."

Jeannette looked troubled. "More calls?"

Molly nodded.

"You told the police?"

"Not yet. I made a note of the times. I doubt if they could have traced them. There wasn't time."

"Maybe you should get one of those call screeners from the phone company. That would tell you the number calling, yes?"

"Jeannette, you're a genius. Why didn't I think of that? I'd forgotten that they'd finally been approved." She dragged out the two volumes of the phone book— *A* to *K* and *L* to *Z*—muttering about the ongoing frustration of always picking the wrong tome to locate a listing. In one moment of absolute fury the previous year, she'd cut apart the white and yellow pages in each volume, then put all the white pages together in one functional book and all the yellow in another. This time, however, she actually found the phone company customer service number on the first try. Within minutes she had arranged for the caller-ID service. By the time she hung up, she was actually looking forward to the next middle-of-the-night call.

After that the day improved considerably. To her astonishment the meeting with Larry Milsap began on time. He breezed in wearing jeans and a flowered Hawaiian shirt, his brown hair pulled back in a ponytail. Despite his inattention to clothes and his maddening disregard for details, he was a genius at production. There was an unmistakable "look" to anything he did on screen. If his talented eye had spotted something special in Brian, Molly was too much the proud mother to disagree. They arranged for a screen test for Brian the following week.

"It's a formality, sweetie. He'll be perfect," Larry said, packing up his briefcase and heading for the door. "The kid already has a mouth on him. I could probably give him the product and let him ad-lib some of that sass, but the agency will provide a script. Thanks, hon. You're an angel."

Molly took the *sweetie, hon,* and *angel* in stride. He was the first person in days who hadn't asked about the murder. By the time he left, she actually thought the day was going pretty well. She ate lunch at her desk, read a script for a producer scheduled to begin shooting in July, and helped Jeannette catch up on the filing. It was nearly four when Vince buzzed her desk. Startled by the unexpected formality, she stuck her head into his office. "What's with you? You usually just shout."

The words were out before she took a good look at his expression. She had seen Vince look smug, sullen and superior, but this was the first time she'd seen him so somber. It somehow answered her question and made her very edgy. She stepped inside.

"What is it?" she asked, standing in front of his

desk, her hands clenching the back of a chair. "Some-thing's the matter, isn't it?"

"Sit down."

His mood was contagious. She suddenly felt very serious herself. "Maybe I ought to stand."

"Suit yourself. I just got off the phone with the county manager."

When he paused to let the significance of that sink in, she prodded, "And? Did he cut our budget? Elimi-nate the entire parks department? What?"

"He says you've been meddling in that murder investigation."

"So?"

"He wants it to stop."

Molly had a hard time accepting the notion that the county manager had nothing better to do in the midst of a near-catastrophic budget crisis than meddle in her private life. "Why does he care?"

"I'm not sure *why* matters. He's the boss."

"Not good enough. What the hell does he expect me to do? Somebody has to look out for my interests. First, I'm considered a suspect. Then somebody starts warning me that I'm in danger. Am I supposed to sit quietly and wait until I become the next victim or land in jail?"

Vince looked startled by that. "Do you honestly think someone might be after you?"

"Vince, I don't know. These calls shake me up. I had more last night that I haven't even told the police about yet. I actually considered tucking a butcher knife under my pillow. Then I thought about Allan Winecroft and decided against it. I figured it might end up in my back."

"Is the caller threatening you?"

"He didn't last night, but it's pretty obvious that someone thinks I know something about the murder."

"All the more reason to sit tight and let the police do their job. I assume they're taking the calls seriously. You want me to call the director?"

She shook her head. "Detective O'Hara was hanging around on an unofficial basis, but he can't be there all the time."

Vince's eyebrows rose. "Maybe he's just using the calls as an excuse to stick close. I've seen the way he looks at you."

"Trust me, the man is all business." There was no need for Vince to know that both she and Michael had recognized the potential for more intimate things developing. At the moment, though, the mysterious Bianca stood squarely between them.

"He's practically engaged," she added for good measure. It was a reminder to her as much as to Vince.

"The woman must love knowing he's hanging out with you."

"I doubt if she's thrilled," Molly admitted. Or maybe she was projecting her own jealousies onto the other woman. Perhaps Bianca was one of those saintly, understanding souls who had enough self-confidence to weather any competition without turning green with envy. Besides, no one had said Molly was any competition, least of all Molly. She'd learned long ago to be careful what she prayed for. She'd once wanted Hal DeWitt and been granted that misguided prayer.

"Maybe she's making the calls," Vince suggested.

"The calls are the reason he's there. I doubt she'd give him an excuse to linger."

"No. No. Maybe she didn't start them, but maybe she's checking up on him now, calling to see if he's around. You know how these possessive chicks get."

"I wouldn't know," she said nobly. "But it doesn't surprise me that you do. Forget this fascination of yours with Michael O'Hara's girl friend for a minute. I'm more interested in figuring out who put a bug in the county manager's ear."

"From what you just said, maybe the girl did it. Benitez did suggest you take a little time off, get away for a while. That'd be a good way to get you out of the picture. He says you have leave coming."

Molly stared at him incredulously. "He checked my personnel records?"

"Apparently so."

Molly finally sat down. "Vince, don't you think that's a little odd? Doesn't the county manager have more important things to worry about than whether I have a few days of leave accumulated?"

"Frankly, I had the feeling he was less concerned about your vacation time than he was about my cutting you loose unless you got your nose out of police business."

"Cutting me loose?" Her voice rose to a shrill tone she didn't recognize. She forced it down. "Does that mean what I think it means?" That, more than a simple phone call, would certainly explain Vince's sober expression.

"You got it. He recommended that I fire you if you didn't cooperate. I told him it was a ridiculous request, that I couldn't let you go without cause, but he wasn't buying. He suggested I try insubordination for starters. I got the feeling more heads would roll if he wasn't satisfied.''

"Meaning yours?" She could feel her hands turn to ice.

Vince shrugged. "There are only so many of us around over here, and he's been looking for an excuse to shake this place up again." He shook his head. "As if last year didn't turn us inside out."

Molly's temper, usually slow to rise, was rapidly reaching the boiling point. She leaped up and headed for the door.

"Where are you going?"

"To get to the bottom of this. I won't let my career, or yours, for that matter, be jeopardized because some jerk downtown is getting pressured."

As she stormed out, she heard Vince's chair crash against the wall. He caught up with her in the parking lot. He was sweating profusely. "Come on, Molly," he coaxed. "You're going to back off, right?"

"That wasn't what I had in mind."

"Come on, you know blowing off steam won't solve anything. Think about it. Look, I'll even buy you and the kid a couple of tickets for California. You could make it a business trip, save the vacation time. Make some contacts, schmooze with the studio execs. Somebody needs to do it soon anyway."

Molly was beyond being cajoled or bribed. "Not on your life. I'm going to find out exactly who is responsible for having the county manager make that call. If I have to, I'll make so much noise the officials at the Metro Building will think they're in the middle of an LA earthquake."

"Oh, shit," Vince murmured, but he didn't try to stop her.

She used her car phone to call police headquarters in search of Michael. It was entirely possible, even after their improved rapport, that he'd decided to exert a little official pressure on her. She didn't think he'd have the gall to suggest that she be fired, but maybe the county manager had simply gotten carried away.

He picked up on the first ring. "O'Hara." His terse tone indicated his mood was about as pleasant as her own.

"I need to see you. I'm on my way."

"Molly?"

If she hadn't been so furious already, she might have considered his insulting failure to recognize her voice as a reason to snap. "Yes," she said tersely. "I'll be there in twenty minutes."

"I'm heading out the door in five. Can't it wait?"

"Unless you're going to investigate the murder of a top county official, no."

"You sound upset," he said cautiously.

"Bingo. No wonder you get so many commendations. Bye."

"Wait. Molly! Molly, are you listening?"

"Yes."

"I'll meet you at the soccer field. The kids have a game in an hour. We should have time to talk. Bring Brian and we'll have dinner after."

"This isn't a social visit," she snapped and hung up.

Molly turned the car toward Kendall. When she reached the field, Michael was lugging soccer equipment from the Jeep to the playing field. He dropped an armload of shin guards and walked slowly back to meet her. When he reached out a hand to touch her, she jerked away. She didn't want the fireworks stirred by his caresses to confuse the issues.

"What's up?" he said, his expression guarded.

"For starters, why are you here instead of chasing down a murderer?"

"I'm pleased you're so concerned about how I spend my days. To answer your question, though, these kids don't have a lot of people they can count on. When I made the commitment, I wanted them to know I wouldn't let them down. Now, why are you here and in such a crappy mood?"

"I've been officially warned to stop meddling in police business."

He dared a smile. When she didn't lighten up, it died. "Okay, what's new about that? I've been begging you to steer clear of the investigation since the day of the murder. You don't pay any attention to me. Why should this be any different?"

"Because this warning carried the clout of the county manager. If I don't behave, I'm out."

"Out? As in fired? Are you sure?"

"Vince was very clear, and for all his flaws, he's loyal. He wouldn't pass along a message like that unless he knew that the county manager meant it and that there was no way out. Did you say something to the director?"

He shoved his hands into his pockets. "You should know me better than that. I don't need officials interfering in my job any more than I need amateurs. I certainly wouldn't say something that would jeopardize your career."

"Maybe you just said something casually, griped to another cop and it escalated, climbed up through the ranks."

"No."

"Have I stepped on some other cop's toes?"

"I'm in charge of the case."

"That doesn't mean someone else couldn't take offense."

"They would have complained to me, not my boss."

"Well, dammit, who's behind this, then?"

Michael looked thoughtful. "Offhand, I'd say the killer. Which leads me to wonder who at Ocean Manor has the ear of the county manager."

Molly stared at him. "Of course. Why didn't I think of that?"

"Because I'm the more obvious choice, and you've probably been itching for a chance to yell at me ever since I left you on Saturday."

"Don't flatter yourself. I didn't give you a thought," she retorted, lying through her teeth, clinging to her pride. "It's true, though, that you were the more approachable choice. As furious as I am, I wasn't looking forward to dashing into the county manager's office for a confrontation without knowing exactly what I'm up against."

Michael's sudden grin was that of a kid just given an opportunity to dunk the principal in a tank of water. "On the other hand, I can hardly wait to butt heads with him," he said.

"Now?" she said enthusiastically.

"Can't do it now. First thing after the game, though. Are you going to stick around and cheer?"

"Why not?" she said agreeably. Michael's promise to take on the county manager was definitely something to cheer about, and she had every intention of being right in the vicinity when he did it. Whether inadvertently or intentionally, someone had first set her up as a murder suspect and now seemed intent on destroying her career. She wasn't going to rest until she'd discovered the culprit and strung him up by his toenails.

She was still trying to think of a fate vile enough for the guilty party when she heard raised voices on the field. More precisely, one raised voice. A woman's. She had her back to Molly, but it was evident from her stance that she was furious. Her hands were jammed in the back pockets of her tight-fitting jeans. Her shoulders were thrown back. Long, shiny dark hair swung with each shouted word directed at Michael. He listened in stoic silence as she ranted. From the tilt of his head, he was gazing at the sky in a *why me* posture.

"You promised that after the game the two of us would be alone for dinner for a change! What good are your promises to me? Why should I ever believe another word?" She waved a hand in the direction of the bleachers. "You bring her here to insult me."

Michael's response was so low, Molly couldn't hear it, but she'd guessed by now that the woman was Bianca and that she was more than upset over Molly's appearance on what she considered her turf. Molly watched with fascination as Michael's jaw tightened. She was surprised that Bianca seemed unconcerned that he was on the verge of exploding. Instead, the woman's clearly provocative words were coming faster now and in Spanish.

Michael shook his head and walked away. Bianca flew after him, stumbling a little as her high heels caught in the grass. A collection of bracelets clinked musically as she grabbed his arm and whirled him around. Molly waited for him to lash back, but if anything, his manner turned gentle. He leaned down and murmured something, soothing her as he might a skittish filly. Bianca suddenly laughed, the fireworks over. He walked her back toward her car, his hand sliding from her waist to her rear. The fond, intimate gesture was almost more than Molly could bear. Michael might say that Bianca had no hold on him, but his actions said otherwise. Suddenly she fully understood the possessive rage that must have surged through Bianca only moments before. Molly had to give her credit. She had given in more gracefully than Molly might have if their positions had been reversed. Then, again, what had Michael promised to soothe her fiery temper?

Michael came back and sat in the row below her on the bleachers, watching as the kids practiced. He kept his back squarely to her.

"Bianca?" she asked finally, staring at the back of his neck. The faint red beneath the tan hinted of tension or embarrassment.

He nodded, his eyes on the field.

"What'd you say to her to set her off?"

"I told her I had to work later."

"She must be used to that. Cops have crazy hours."

"I told her I wouldn't be home."

Molly's pulse bucked, then raced. "No wonder she was furious." Hallelujah!

"She'll live. I'm not so sure about you."

Lusty thoughts screeched to a halt. Molly swallowed hard as he turned an intense look on her. "I'm serious," he said. "I've got a feeling about this. I can always tell when a case is about to break wide open. I'm not letting you out of my sight until all the pieces fall into place and the right person is behind bars."

Molly couldn't tear her gaze away from the look in his eyes. The emotion was too raw. "You could have someone else stand guard."

"No," he said quietly as he stood up to go back to the game. "We're going to ride this out together."

If the rest of the night was any indication, it was going to be a hell of a ride.

Michael called all over until he finally tracked down the county manager at his home. While Molly listened on the extension, he demanded to know to whom he'd been talking about the case. Roberto Benitez tried playing coy.

"I thought this was what you wanted, *amigo*. It came from the department that the DeWitt woman was getting in your way and on your nerves."

"I know better," Michael said. "My superiors and I haven't had a single conversation regarding Mrs. De-Witt's actions beyond the fact that she might be a witness."

"And a suspect," the manager added. "Is that not true?"

"Very low on the list."

"Then I think I am being generous in merely

warning her. I could have suspended her for the dura-
tion of the investigation."

"I want to know exactly who involved you in this,"
Michael repeated. "You can tell me now or we can do
it officially."

There was a long silence while Benitez considered
the effect an official inquiry might have on his political
fortunes. He served at the whim of some very fickle
commissioners.

"I had several calls," he conceded finally.

"From?"

"The victim's wife spoke to my wife, as a matter of
fact."

"And? I don't believe for a minute that you'd take
this kind of action based on some indirect comment
from Mrs. Winecroft."

"Mr. Gonzalez also spoke to me, as well as Mr.
Mendoza," he said with obvious reluctance. "It seems
your witness has offended a number of important people."

"And now I'm offended," Michael retorted. "You
know what happens when I get offended, don't you? I
tend to start asking some very hard questions. I wonder why certain people find a need to come to you. I
wonder if they're trying to protect their own asses. And
I get really uptight that a county official might help
them to do that."

"Detective, I have tolerated quite a lot from you in
the past." The manager's voice was icy. "Do not step
over the line."

"I might say the same to you. Good night," he
said, then added as a pointedly derisive afterthought,
"sir."

When he'd hung up, Molly walked back into the living room. "I guess it's a good thing I'm going to that luncheon tomorrow."

His thoughts clearly still on the call, Michael asked distractedly, "What luncheon is that?"

"It's honoring Drucilla."

He glanced up from his notes. "Exactly how is that supposed to help?"

"Mrs. Benitez, Mrs. Mendoza, and Drucilla all in the same room. Surely I can get a few clues about the men in their lives from that little scenario. Care to come along?"

He actually shuddered. "Not if they paid me."

"And I thought we were going to stick together like glue," she said, feigning disappointment. Actually, she was delighted she was going to have a chance at those three women all on her own. Having Michael breathing down her neck would have definitely cramped her style.

"I'm not sure I'm crazy about this," he said.

"I'll be fine," she said, filled with bravado from her previous investigative successes. "They're not likely to take me out at a charity luncheon. I promise, though, if any of them reach for the butter knife, I'll cut and run."

Michael looked more worried than ever. "Don't make light of this, Molly. We're not playing a game."

"Believe me, no one is taking this any more seriously than I am. My whole future seems to hinge on the outcome. Jailhouse gray would be lousy with my complexion."

"I'd be more worried about the alternative, if I were you."

CHAPTER
FOURTEEN

Five hundred women, wearing vibrant spring colors and sipping mimosas, were wondering whether Drucilla Winecroft would dare to show up at the latest luncheon in her honor. If the committee members had been taking bets instead of selling raffle tickets, they would have scored a record haul.

Dozens of cocktail parties for film industry officials, plus more than her share of cotillions, had made Molly something of an expert at mingling at packed-to-the-walls occasions like this. As soon as she'd registered and paid for her ticket, she moved from cluster to cluster, smiling, listening, then slipping away without commenting on much more than the weather outside and the clothes in the room. The former was beastly, the latter stylish and expensive. She could have traveled to Europe on what a couple of the designer outfits must have cost. There was no need for a fashion show at this event. The spring collections of the country's top designers were represented right in the room.

According to Molly's unofficial tally, Drucilla was favored to appear, if only to prove that she wasn't behind bars.

Sympathy was also on the widow's side. There wasn't a woman in the room who didn't think that a satin-lined box was too good for the man who'd cheated on the ever-charming cultural benefactress. Feeding Allan to the sharks was the disposal method of choice. Since he was already in the ground, it was a belated thought.

During her first tour of the room, Molly had spotted the wives of several area mayors and chairwomen from at least ten other events she'd received invitations to during the course of the year. Drucilla had served on all the committees. It was payback time.

To her disappointment, though, Molly had yet to spot any of the women she'd hoped to see. Mrs. Benitez was short, so it was entirely possible that she was hidden from view in the center of the crush. Rosa Mendoza, however, was tall and a stately size sixteen. She tended to dominate a room, in the most positive sense of the word. Molly had watched her walk into a ballroom once. Every head in the room had turned toward the force of her radiant smile, like flowers seeking sunshine. It had been an astonishing display. A woman like that would be an unmistakable asset to her husband. Molly wondered if Manny Mendoza deserved her. For Rosa's sake only, she hoped she was wrong about his possible involvement in some sort of cover-up attempt. His call to the county manager was suspicious, as far as Molly was concerned.

A chime sounded, signaling the start of the luncheon. Slowly, amid much laughter and the mingled scents of a dozen designer perfumes, the women began to enter the Intercontinental's waterfront ballroom with its spectacular view of the bay. Molly stayed by the center door, her eyes peeled on the crowd as the women passed by.

Finally, Mrs. Benitez, whom she'd met at several official county functions, appeared, all of her attention focused on the woman at her side. Molly stepped in front of her, smiled, and managed to inject a note of enthusiasm into her greeting. Startled, Mrs. Benitez faltered, then regained her aplomb. "Why, hello. Molly, isn't it?"

"Yes, it's so nice to see you again."

"Do you know Mrs. Jackson? This is Molly . . ." She hesitated.

"DeWitt," Molly supplied.

The county manager's wife suddenly appeared nervous. "Of course. I should have remembered."

"Yes, you and Drucilla were discussing me just the other day, I hear."

Mrs. Benitez tried subtly to scurry behind her guest, but Molly was able to get between them. "Why, yes," she said, glancing around with a desperate look in her eyes. "I believe she did mention you were neighbors."

"And that I'd found her husband's body?" Molly inquired politely. Mrs. Jackson gasped. Resigned that there was no escaping Molly's determination, Mrs. Benitez took the announcement with admirable calm.

"I suppose that might have come up. If you'll excuse us, we really should find our table."

Molly beamed again and stepped aside. "Certainly." She'd found out exactly what she'd been looking for. Drucilla had made that call to the county manager's wife. If she could just locate Rosa Mendoza now, she'd consider the day a success, even if she had to eat rubbery chicken for lunch.

With nearly everyone seated, there didn't seem to be much hope of spotting the developer's wife without weaving in and out among the fifty-five tables with their towering centerpieces of pink tulips reportedly imported from Amsterdam. With waiters already crowding the aisles, Molly resigned herself to going to her own table. Since she'd made her reservation late and alone, she'd been relegated to a table at the back of the room. The better to observe, she told herself, just as Rosa Mendoza swept down on her in a rustle of bright-red silk.

"Molly, I thought I saw you earlier, but in this mob, who can tell. I saw your name at the registration desk. You are alone, yes?"

"Yes. I didn't know until the last minute that I'd be able to make it. I didn't want to miss it. Drucilla's been through so much. She deserves this day of recognition."

Rosa nodded sympathetically. "You are right and it is a lovely party, isn't it? You will come to my table, *sí*? I had a cancellation just this morning. There is a place. It has been a long time since we have had a chance to chat. It is so funny that now we are neighbors, I never seem to see you. We have much to catch up on."

"We do," Molly agreed. Perfect.

Rosa's table was crowded with women whose hus-

bands did business with Manny. Many of them, in their
own right, held important jobs or led major fund-rais-
ing efforts for various charities, but Molly was more
fascinated by the connections to the developer. His
name crept into the conversation at frequent intervals,
always with the faintest edge of reverence.

Molly turned to the woman on her left, who was
wearing a marquise diamond the size of a peach pit.
"Your husband works with Manny?"

"Yes. They, how do you say, developed? Yes, developed many properties together. Hernando says Manny
is a genius."

Rosa leaned over. "Don't let him hear you say
that, please. I have much trouble carving his ego down
to size as it is."

"He must be incredibly busy," Molly said.

"Always," Rosa lamented. "All he ever thinks of is
work, work, work. Now that the children are grown, he
is worse than ever."

"How did he find the time for the condominium
association?" Molly wondered aloud.

"He said it was his duty. He created the property.
It is where we live."

"Manny developed Ocean Manor?"

"*Sí.* It is, what is the expression, the jewel in his
crown."

No wonder the man thought he would hold the
throne indefinitely. Would his loss in the last election
have made him so resentful that he would kill? Tonight's condominium association meeting would give
Molly a chance to see the man in action. Maybe that
would tell her if he was capable of murder.

Meantime, though, Drucilla had just been intro-

duced to a standing ovation. The queen lived. Long
live the queen!

• • •

Despite the thunder outside the rumble of discontent
was evident long before Molly reached the meeting
room. The emergency session of the Ocean Manor
Board of Directors hadn't even started and already residents were sniping. If it weren't for her curiosity
about who would emerge victorious in the latest quest
for power, she'd have stayed home to watch *Jeopardy!*
and then her favorite, the complex mystery puzzles of
Matlock. She had a feeling tonight's live entertainment
was going to be more akin to mud wrestling.

She slid into the back of the packed and already
airless room and found the last vacant chair in the last
row. Michael spotted her, inched his way through the
crowd and leaned down to whisper, "Welcome to the
Tuesday night fights."

Molly tried to ignore the way his hand rested on
her shoulder, but she liked the sensation too much.
"Already?" she said as his fingers began a gentle mas-
sage. She felt her own tension begin to drain away.
"The meeting hasn't even started."

"They've been battling over who gets to sit in the
front row."

Actually, Molly decided after a few minutes' observation, the tense atmosphere was only slightly worse
than last Tuesday night's battle between the Winecrofts. "Let's just hope this week's version doesn't
culminate in another murder," she murmured. Michael's caress ended and she sighed.

As condo vice president Boris Yankovich gaveled

the meeting to order, Tyler Jenkins wrested control of the floor microphone away from another speaker. "I'd like to say something."

He was immediately drowned out by catcalls from the audience. Boris moved ahead as if the older man hadn't spoken at all. "Ladies and gentlemen, we have to make a few decisions tonight."

It was evident that the ladies and gentlemen in question were seated at the head table, not in the audience. Not once did the vice president deign to glance in their direction.

He went on. "Due to the unfortunate death of our president, it is necessary that we move to fill that seat on the board. It has been recommended that we expedite that process by appointing a man whose vast experience more than qualifies him to step in, Mr. Manny Mendoza."

Molly's mouth dropped open in astonishment. "They can't do that."

Michael stared at her. "Why not?"

"The bylaws call for an election to fill any unexpired term with more than a year remaining. Allan was just elected to a two-year term a few months ago."

"They must know that."

"If not, Jack Kingsley should have told them. He's the one who told me."

Tyler was shaking his fist at the head table. "That's illegal," he shouted. His words were emphasized by another powerful clap of thunder.

"You're out of order, Mr. Jenkins," Boris said. He turned to the others. "Could I have a motion regarding Mr. Mendoza?"

Gerry Wilson waved a hand. "So moved."

"Second," Katie Winslow said.

"Discussion," Boris said, carrying on the mockery in an orderly fashion.

"Why do you bother paying an attorney?" Tyler shouted, not even bothering with the microphone. A few daring souls murmured agreement. None stood up. Jack Kingsley stood off to the side, rocking back on his heels and staring at the ceiling. Manny Mendoza was seated in the first row, briefcase in hand, the epitome of a man ready to get to work. Rosa had not come down to witness the coronation.

Molly kept waiting for someone to speak up and stop this charade. When no one budged, she started forward. Michael grabbed for her arm, but she shook him off. When she was halfway down the aisle, she caught sight of Liza's upturned face. With a subtle shake of her head, she gave Molly a warning, but Molly was too livid to be called off now. As the directors conferred in undertones, their hands discreetly over their own microphones, she tapped Tyler on the shoulder and gestured him aside. His ashen complexion alarmed her. "Sit for a minute," she whispered. "Let me try to get through to them."

Surprised by the unexpected backing, he nodded and sank onto one of the metal chairs.

"Excuse me," Molly said in a tone that carried to the back of the room. It was a skill she'd learned in elocution classes. At long last she'd found a use for it. The sound echoed as she waited. Slowly the room fell silent. The directors raised their heads and stared at her, obviously startled by her daring interruption.

"Why are you doing this?" she asked. "Each one of you has to know that the bylaws of this building require that there be an election process. Isn't that right, Mr. Kingsley? That is what you told me, isn't it?''

His slouched shoulders straightened. "Yes, ma'am. I believe I did. However, there are certain provisions, in an emergency, for bypassing that procedure. You can rest assured that we've checked all of this out with an attorney.''

"Why would you want to, though? Why not give the residents the opportunity to speak out in the election they're entitled to?''

Even as she said it, she thought she knew the answer. For some reason this board wanted—possibly even needed—Manny Mendoza. They weren't willing to risk another election in which he might lose. Why? What had Allan discovered? What had he been on the verge of revealing when he was murdered?

Molly knew she couldn't very well stand up there and accuse the board, much less Mendoza himself, of doing something illegal. They'd have her in court charged with slander before the words were out of her mouth. Mendoza at least was powerful enough to make the charge stick, even if truth were on her side. That would also make him powerful enough to reach the county manager as well.

Caught up in her new theory, she murmured a few more wasted words and hurried to the back of the room where Michael waited, his dark eyes alternately surveying the crowd and watching her.

"Pretty gutsy stuff for a woman whose life already might be in danger," he said. His tone wasn't entirely complimentary. He took a closer look. "Are you okay?''

By way of an answer Molly dragged him outside the room.

"I think we've spent too much time worrying about the Winecrofts' marital problems," she said as they went back to her apartment. "From everything we've heard, those have been going on for a long time. There was no real reason for either one of them to turn violent all of a sudden. So what did change the last few months?"

Michael caught her train of thought at once. "Allan's election to the board."

"Right. I'm willing to bet that he stumbled onto some deep dark secret and that it has something to do with Mendoza."

"But if Mendoza's the one mixed up in something shady, why would Drucilla and Gonzalez have called the county manager into this?"

"I think they're trying to protect each other. Neither of them is willing to admit the possibility that the other might be guilty of Allan's murder. If they'd just be honest and get everything out in the open about that night, I doubt they'd have any more worries on that score. Can't you just call Mendoza in for questioning?"

He shook his head. "I don't have the first real shred of evidence against the man. The most I could do would be to have an unofficial chat. You can just imagine how fast news of that visit would reach the county manager's ear."

Seated in Molly's dining room, they were still debating the best course of action when they heard a knock at the door.

"I'll get it," Brian shouted, already running from

his room. "It's probably Kevin. He was gonna come over to play video games." He threw open the door. "Oh, my gosh! Mom! Mom, there's a lady at the door and she's got a knife!"

CHAPTER
FIFTEEN

Brian had sounded more fascinated than scared by the knife, but that wasn't Molly's reaction. She responded with a primal surge of terror, maternal instincts churning. She was on her feet and running, but even so it took only a half dozen of Michael's long-legged strides to beat her to the door. He had one hand under the lapel of his jacket and on the handle of his gun. His jaw was tensed, but other than that he appeared astonishingly cool and calm as he faced Drucilla Winecroft across the threshold.

"Back away, son," he said quietly. Molly wanted to scream. Then she saw Drucilla's expression. She was staring at Michael's gun in absolute terror.

"What is it?" she said, her voice quavering. "I haven't done anything."

"The knife," Michael said. "Hand it to me. Slowly."

"You're acting as if . . . Oh, my Lord, I see. You

thought . . . How terrible. Brian, sweetie, Molly, I'm so sorry if I scared you. I was just returning your things. With everything that's happened, I forgot I had them. I took them upstairs after the bridge game."

Understanding dawned in Michael's wary gaze. He nodded toward Molly. "These are yours?"

Finally Molly was able to drag her eyes away from her son long enough to take a good look at what Drucilla was carrying. Tucked under her arm was Molly's glass cake plate with the calla lily pattern. In her hand was the knife Molly had taken to the fateful bridge game. She knew it was hers because of the deep scratches in the handle. They had happened one night when the knife had slid, accidentally, handle first into the garbage disposal, creating the worst racket she'd ever heard. On the morning of the murder she'd never gotten close enough to actually see if the handle had similar scars.

"They're mine," she confirmed. "But I don't understand. I thought . . ." Her gaze rose to meet Michael's. "The murder weapon wasn't mine after all."

"Which explains why there was only one set of prints, the murderer's, not yours. Shit. I'd better call the lab. We should have picked up on something like this that first day."

Molly invited Drucilla in and fixed her a cup of coffee, while they waited for Michael to get off the phone with the police lab. His terse orders crackled with impatience.

"They'll try to get back to me tonight."

"Why has it taken so long? Was the lab backed up?" Molly asked.

"Some nitwit didn't see the need to rush because

somebody mentioned the prints were yours." He turned to Drucilla. "Mrs. Winecroft, have you given any more thought to what we discussed the other day? Did your husband have any enemies who might have made those anonymous calls?"

Drucilla sat at the table and leaned forward intently. "Detective, as you may have surmised by now, my husband was not a particularly kind or generous man. He was a perfectionist, and like all perfectionists he made his share of enemies. When he was running my father's company, he was despised by the workers because he wouldn't tolerate mistakes. The board, however, found no fault, because under his guidance the company was more profitable and respected than ever before."

"I'm not sure I understand what that might have to do with the murder," Michael said.

Drucilla looked as if she didn't believe for a second that Michael's comprehension was the least bit slow. She answered anyway. "I'm afraid he ran this condominium the same way. He was putting pressure on everyone to make improvements in efficiency, to cut back the excess spending. Tyler knew how Allan was. Tyler held a seat on the company's board for years. He was a friend of my father's. We found our apartment while visiting him several years ago. At any rate, because he knew Allan's style so well, he encouraged him to run for the condo board. He was fed up with the lax business decisions being made around here."

"So while Allan was making improvements and cutting costs, he was doing it with a heavy hand?" Michael said.

"Absolutely. He was not the sort of businessman to care about making friends, as long as he improved the bottom line."

"You don't think he cared about the effect this had on people?" Molly said, trying to understand how anyone could totally separate the two issues. "What about Enrique, for instance? He'd worked here as a security guard since the building opened. He had a large family to support. Obviously, he'd been doing things the same way for years. Shouldn't Allan have given him a chance to change, or at least to explain?"

"If you're asking what I think, yes, he should have. Allan wouldn't see it that way. He saw things in terms of right and wrong, perfection and mistakes. He'd told the guards they were to log in every single nonresident car, and he wasn't beyond checking to see that they did. That's what happened with Enrique. One of Allan's cronies came over. Enrique recognized him and let him in and didn't write it down. Allan happened to check the log later that day. The visit wasn't there. He fired Enrique. For Allan, it was a simple matter. The man hadn't followed a direct order. I spoke with Enrique after that myself and offered to help him and his family in any way I could."

"You did?" Michael said.

"Of course. We had known the man for years. I occasionally hired him to tend bar at our parties. I told him I would help see that he got more of those jobs."

He ought to do very well, Molly thought. Drucilla's friends gave a lot of parties.

"What was his reaction?" Michael asked.

"He sounded very grateful. Enrique is a very gracious, polite man. That's why I've used him so often. He makes a lovely impression on the guests."

Molly had a sudden thought. "Do other residents hire him as well?"

"Certainly," Drucilla said. "I've recommended him very highly."

Michael nodded. "You're thinking that he might have had access to the knife, right?"

"It makes sense, doesn't it? We know the killer must have had a knife just like mine."

"But there's only one way the killer could have known to use the matching knife," Michael said slowly. "He had to have been in the cardroom that night. Was Enrique in the building? Would he have any reason to want to set you up? Is he even clever enough to try, or was it just an accident that the weapon matched your knife?"

"Are you speculating aloud or asking me?" Molly said. "If I knew all that, I'd ask for a transfer to the Metro police force."

Michael grinned. "Let's take it one at a time then. Was he here the night of the murder?"

"I didn't see him," Molly said. "Drucilla? Was anyone having a party that night? That's the only way he could have gotten on the grounds."

"Unless he told the man on duty he'd just come back to collect some of his things," Michael said. "If it was a guard he knew, he wouldn't have been questioned."

Molly shook her head. "The guard on the gate that night was new. He'd probably had all of the rules drilled into his head. In fact, he probably knew that letting an unauthorized person in was exactly what had gotten Enrique fired in the first place. It had to be a party. Was anyone having one that night, Drucilla?''

"None of our friends, but the log at the desk would indicate if anyone had a lot of guests in or if anyone held something in the party room.''

"I'll call the desk,'' Molly offered, though she was certain she already knew the answer. The logs she'd seen had had no more than the usual number of drop-by visitors registered.

"Don't bother,'' Michael said. "I had all the logs taken to headquarters as evidence. I'll call over there in a minute. Let's get back to those other questions. How did you get along with Enrique, Molly? Was he holding any sort of grudge against you?''

"Absolutely not. In fact, he came by my office to talk after he got fired. I gave him the county job listings in case there was something he was qualified to do.''

"Was he angry enough at Allan to kill him?''

"No.''

"You sound certain.''

"I am. If anything, he was hurt. He couldn't understand why anyone would do that to him after all those years.''

Drucilla agreed. "He said as much when I talked to him, too.''

"So, even if he had the motive and the opportunity, neither of you think he was capable of plotting Allan's murder, implicating Molly, and going through with it.''

"Capable in the sense of being bright enough, maybe,'' Molly said. "He had some sort of graduate degree in Cuba, but it took him a long time in this country to learn the language. Whatever his field was, it required some sort of licensing, and I guess he never felt confident enough in his English to try for it.''

"Even so, he's not your top suspect, right?''

"No," Molly agreed. Drucilla nodded.

Michael sat back and sighed heavily. "Which brings us right back where we were. We've got suspects all over the place, some with motive but no apparent opportunity, some with opportunity but no obvious motive.''

"I'm sorry I wasn't more help," Drucilla said.

She looked as though she couldn't quite make up her mind whether to go or stay. Molly had the feeling she didn't really want to return to an empty apartment. "Why don't I pour you another cup of coffee,'' she suggested. "Maybe if we all put our heads together we can narrow things down a little.''

"Good idea," Michael said.

"Are you sure?'' Drucilla said.

"Absolutely,'' Molly said, going into the kitchen to make more coffee. Michael was right on her heels. He nudged her aside and took over the coffee-making duty.

"Yours is too weak,'' he said. "Sissy stuff. What did you think in there? For a woman who just lost her husband in a violent murder doesn't she seem oddly calm to you?''

"If the man was such a petty tyrant, plus a womanizer, she's probably relieved, especially if she wants to marry Juan Gonzalez.''

"But you really don't think she's guilty, do you?''

Molly considered the possibility, trying to separate gut instinct from fact. "God knows she had the motive and the opportunity, but for some reason I just don't think so—for all those reasons we were discussing right before she came. I'm more convinced than ever we should check out Mendoza. Besides, if Drucilla had done it, I just can't imagine that she'd want to hang around with you any longer than absolutely necessary."

"Maybe it's my charm."

"You may be irresistible to most women, but . . ."

"Including you?" he interrupted.

"Don't fish for compliments."

"Interesting."

"What?"

"You're nervous."

"I am not."

"Then why are you pouring salt into the coffee?"

Molly's gaze jerked to the container in her hand. It was sugar. "You really are obnoxious, Detective."

"Because I was right?"

"You weren't right. It was sugar, not salt."

"Ah, but your reaction told me you weren't one bit certain of that. Only someone who's already rattled would have needed to look."

"Is that some strange police technique for determining guilt or innocence?"

"It has its uses."

She couldn't imagine that he would look any more smug if he'd just solved the case. Molly decided right then against continuing an argument she couldn't win. The man did make her nervous. It always made her nervous being attracted to a man who was already spoken for, especially when he was sending out signals that weren't all that clear-cut. A devoted lover wouldn't be camping on her doorstep. He'd be home in his own bed with Bianca.

Or would he? Michael wouldn't be the first Latin male of her acquaintance to court one woman while living with or married to another. Something told Molly, though, that Michael had more scruples than that, probably because of his own irregular parental situation. And attraction aside, Michael was a damned good cop. He would never let his personal situation get between him and what he considered to be his duty.

Duty! The thought that he might classify her as no more than that depressed her.

"As I was saying," she said firmly, "I doubt murderers would risk revealing their guilt no matter how charming they might find you on a personal level. Drucilla's not budging, ergo she's innocent."

"I have to admit, my money's on someone else, too. Damn, I wish the lab would call back. I'd love to get a match on those fingerprints."

Just as they started back toward the dining room, where Drucilla was waiting, the front door burst open. Since she'd heard the key in the lock an instant before, Molly knew it was Liza, but Michael couldn't have guessed that. For the second time that night his body tensed. His hand was within inches of his gun.

Liza spotted the automatic gesture and skidded to a halt. "You don't need the damned gun," she said quietly, "but if you're any good at CPR, you'd better get out to the pool. There's a woman floating facedown. From my balcony it looks as though she's dead."

CHAPTER
SIXTEEN

The woman found floating facedown in the clear turquoise pool, blond hair streaming, was Ingrid Nielsen. Although security guards had materialized instantly at Liza's frantic calls for help, by the time Molly and Michael reached the pool it was clearly too late for their energetic attempts at CPR. Michael checked to be sure, as did the doctor from the seventh floor. She was dead, sprawled on the rain-dampened concrete in a revealing bikini. The air was thick with humidity and hushed speculation. Molly kept thinking that someone ought to cover her up.

Michael tried to clear the scene of the crowd that had gathered, but it was impossible. Because of the condo meeting, more people than usual were out and about at this late hour. They moved back, but not inside. The sad part, Molly observed, was that no one seemed to be mourning Ingrid. They were too busy wondering aloud about how she'd died, which one among them might be a murderer, and the effect this was likely to have on property values. Putting priorities in order and sensing panic, one of the island's top real estate agents was trying to reassure them that island condos would always bring top dollar. No one seemed to believe her.

"Mom." Brian's voice shook and his lower lip quivered. Molly had told him to stay upstairs. Naturally he hadn't. "Is she dead?"

"Yes." Worried about him, she steered him as far from the scene as she could, until the width of the pool and several people were between them and Ingrid's body.

"Did somebody kill her, too?"

"I'm not sure about that. We'll have to wait for the police to decide how she died."

"The police are lousy," he said, glaring at Michael on the other side of the pool, where he was organizing the crime scene investigators. "He promised to protect you. If he couldn't protect her, how can he take care of you?"

"Maybe he didn't know she needed protecting," Molly said slowly. Everyone had assumed that Allan's death was a single act of passion, that he'd been targeted because of his marital infidelities or his abrasive personality or the discovery of someone's dirty little secret.

Who, then, would have wanted Ingrid dead? Certainly at one time, Drucilla might have hated her enough to kill her, but now? With Allan dead, the affair was certainly over and Drucilla already had Juan anyway. For her, murdering Ingrid would be more or less redundant. Besides, Drucilla had been upstairs with them since before the storm ended. Surely that eliminated her as a suspect.

Molly tried to calculate the time of death to be sure. She hadn't seen Ingrid at the condo meeting. As a renter, she wouldn't have needed to be there. That sudden, intense storm had ended about an hour ago. Ingrid wouldn't have gone for a swim while it was still lightning and thundering. If she'd gone earlier, someone would have noticed the body much sooner. It made more sense that she'd been killed just minutes ago, right after the pool lights went off at ten. With the scudding clouds still overhead, it was unlikely anyone would have seen the murder, especially if she'd been knocked unconscious in the shadows, then tossed in the pool to drown. Liza had seen the body only because a distant flash of lightning had momentarily illuminated it.

If Molly was right about all that, Drucilla was out as a suspect. It was more likely that Ingrid had known something, the same something that had gotten Allan stabbed. Or she might have guessed the identity of the killer. Perhaps the two pieces of information went hand in hand. If Allan had known someone's secret, and if he had shared that information with Ingrid, then it was entirely likely that the killer had figured out that she was a danger to him too. Then, *bam,* there she was in the pool.

Not for one single second did Molly consider that it might be an accidental drowning. The odds that this was nothing more than coincidence were probably greater than those of being the only person to pick all six numbers in the Florida lottery. As for suicide, there were easier ways than trying to stay underwater long enough to die.

"Wait here," she told Brian. "I need to see Michael for a minute. I'll send Liza over here to wait with you. Okay?"

Brian put on a very brave face. "Sure, Mom."

She found Liza, then located Michael with the crime scene specialists. "Can I see you for a minute?"

"Now?"

"It has to do with the murders."

"Murders?"

"Don't be coy. You may not have the evidence yet, but you know as well as I do that she didn't throw herself in here because she was distraught over losing Allan. She thought she'd just struck it rich."

"Maybe she found out she wasn't mentioned in the will."

Molly hesitated. "Did she?"

"I don't know. I'm speculating, which is what you're doing."

"I like mine better. I think you ought to check her apartment."

"We'll get to it."

"Now," she said.

His gaze narrowed. "Why?"

"I think she knew something about Allan's death, either who killed him or the information he had that got him killed, which is pretty much the same thing."

He nodded slowly. "Okay. Could be. What is it you think we'll find in the apartment?"

"Okay, let's say Allan had told her something, late-night pillow talk and all that. Now, I'm still working on this part, but what if she said something to somebody at the pool, something overheard by the killer that let him know she'd figured it out. He couldn't very well let it go, could he?"

"No, but what's in the apartment?"

"A note, a name, I don't know. I just think you ought to check it out."

"We will."

"Now, dammit."

"Why the urgency? Shouldn't you be with Brian?"

"He's fine. Liza's with him. Now let's go. If I'm right, the killer's going to be up there looking for whatever she had too."

To her relief Michael nodded at last. It was a testament to the fact that he valued her opinion. He turned to one of the uniformed officers. "I'm going to check out her apartment." He motioned to Nestor. "I'll need a master key."

"*Sí, sí.*" The security chief pulled a ring with keys of every size and shape from his pocket as he hurried toward the building.

Upstairs, it took Nestor only two tries to find the right key for Ingrid's deadbolt lock. Seeing Molly's astonished expression, he said, "Is master key, *sí*? Must be on master or provide with copy for emergency. Pipes burst. Fire, maybe. You see?"

"I see," Molly agreed as Michael stepped into the apartment. She heard his muttered expletive before she got a good look inside.

"What?" she said.

He stepped aside. "See for yourself."

The apartment had been ransacked. If she hadn't seen the taut set of Michael's lips, she might have been tempted to gloat.

"Who else has a set of keys like yours?" Michael asked Nestor.

"The man in charge each shift, the chief engineer, the office."

"Michael, they wouldn't have needed a master key," Molly said. "She probably had her own keys with her at the pool when she was attacked. The killer could have taken those."

Michael radioed down to poolside. "Any sign of her apartment keys down there?"

"I'll check," the officer said. "No. Just a towel, sandals and some sort of T-shirt."

"What about pinned to her bathing suit? Sometimes swimmers do that, so they won't have to leave the key lying around."

"I'll check again, but I don't think so."

"Thanks, Marty. I'll be in the apartment awhile. When you guys finish down there, I need you up here."

"Ten-four."

Molly walked slowly around the apartment, paying particular attention to the places where the most damage had been done. It was hard to differentiate, actually. The whole place was a mess. Molly tried to put herself in Ingrid's shoes. Where would she have hidden something as important as a clue to Allan's murderer?

"Don't touch anything," Michael warned.

"I know. I just wish I knew exactly what I was looking for," she said as she went into the kitchen. By the phone she found a pad with several numbers scribbled on it, all with the island's 361 prefix. "Michael, do you have a notebook with you?"

He came to the door. "Sure. What did you find?"

"Just a bunch of phone numbers. Could be neighbors or stores."

"Or one of them could be the killer's." He copied the numbers down. "We'll call from downstairs."

Molly was ready to call right then, but didn't dare touch the phone. She used a corner of her blouse and one finger to pull open drawers and cabinets, but found absolutely nothing except the usual assortment of dishes, glassware, and pots and pans. There were no small kitchen appliances, not even a mixer. The refrigerator was nearly bare. A carton of milk, three containers of yogurt, and a chunk of cheese were on one shelf. Greasy residue from past groceries was on all the rest. There were two apples in the produce drawer. Apparently Ingrid had not been expected to cook for Allan. That made it all the more likely that at least some of those phone numbers were for local carry-out restaurants.

Molly moved on to the broom closet, which held a surprisingly complete stock of cleansers, polishers, brooms, and mops. Either Ingrid had preferred cleaning to cooking or she'd had a maid who insisted on being well equipped. Molly thought of the petite housekeeper she'd seen at the Winecroft apartment. Surely Allan hadn't been tacky enough to insist that the two women in his life share a maid. Of course, neither apartment was so outrageously large that one housekeeper couldn't have managed both as long as no meals were required. She already knew that the Winecrofts always ate out. She resolved to have another chat with Conchita as soon as she finished in here.

She wrapped a dishcloth around her hand and patted along the top shelf to make sure there was nothing there except dust cloths. Suddenly she felt something flat and hard underneath.

Uncertain what to do next, she called for Michael. He reappeared in the door at once. "What?"

"I think I found something. Can I take it out?"

"Use a cloth."

"I'll just wrap it in the dustcloths, okay?"

He nodded.

She folded the cloths around whatever Ingrid had hidden beneath them and pulled it out, then laid it on the counter. Michael used his pen to lift away the layers of cloth. A knife fell out. It was a large, lethal-looking carving knife.

"Why would she hide a carving knife in the broom closet?" Michael said, but Molly knew. Though the blade wasn't serrated, this knife came from the same set as the original murder weapon. She had one just like it in her kitchen.

"Don't you see," she said. "She knew the killer. This knife came from the same set. We already know there was a second set, because Drucilla just returned my knife. Ingrid figured it out, too. She must have been in someone's apartment and seen it."

"Or it was hers and she realized it could be incriminating."

"She wouldn't have a knife like this," Molly said with absolute certainty. "They're very expensive. She doesn't even cook."

"How can you tell?"

"I checked the refrigerator. The woman lived on dairy products. Her cholesterol was probably awful.

Nope, I'm convinced she found the knife in the killer's apartment.''

"There could be a dozen sets just like this in this building alone.''

"Maybe, but only one of them is missing two knives.''

"The killer could have had them replaced by now.''

Molly shook her head. "He'd have to buy a complete set. Then he'd have extra knives he couldn't explain.''

"So why not just throw out the set? Bingo, no incriminating knives at all.''

"Because Ingrid already had this one. It probably has fingerprints on it, just like the murder weapon.''

"Right,'' Michael said, looking impressed with her reasoning. Being taken seriously was heady stuff for a woman whose husband had belittled everything she said. "I'll send it to the lab. I don't get it, though. Why wouldn't she turn it over to us in the first place? She must have wanted Allan's killer caught.''

"I have a theory about that,'' Molly admitted.

"I'm sure.''

She scowled at him. "Do you want to hear this or not?''

"Please.''

"Okay. What if she'd been left out of Allan's will? Obviously she liked her lifestyle here. She had no source of income that we know of. She finds the knife, maybe some other evidence on the killer and decides to blackmail him. Chances are it's someone who has money, and clearly it's someone who doesn't want his or her secrets broadcast to the world.''

"You've been reading too damned many scripts."

"Admit it," she said. "It's possible."

He grinned. "I didn't say they were bad scripts. Let's check her bank records."

They found her checkbook in her purse. Her balance was a scanty $24.87. Michael whistled as he discovered a deposit slip for $10,000.00 in cash. The money, however, was missing, taken, no doubt, by the killer.

"If I'd known blackmail could be that lucrative around here, even I might have been tempted into a life of crime," she said.

"So who on our list of suspects has the kind of cash to even fake a payoff like that?"

"Not me."

"You were at the bottom anyway."

"Thank you."

"You're welcome. Now who does?"

"Drucilla certainly. And Mendoza. Tyler Jenkins, I guess. Not the Davisons and probably not Roy Meeks. Certainly not the security guard. I like Mendoza. For some reason he really liked the power of the presidency."

"Or the kickbacks. If there was a lot of mismanagement going on, he'd probably been getting his cut to turn a blind eye to it."

"And his wife's a gourmet cook. I'd forgotten all about that until now. The paper did a big spread once on some of her recipes. She could very well have a set of knives just like these."

"Let's go pay them a visit, then."

"You'll let me tag along?" she said, surprised.

"If I don't, you'll probably try to climb onto the balcony so you can hear."

"I would never do that."

"Right."

Since his skepticism was working in her behalf, and since the Mendozas lived on the penthouse floor, Molly decided not to mention that she was terrified of heights. Even on her own lower balcony, she never went near the railing. Occasionally she tested herself by inching close to the edge. Each time she was struck by such an attack of vertigo she had to retreat immediately. As long as she stayed inside at the Mendozas', though, she ought to be just fine.

Unfortunately they weren't at home. They hadn't been at the pool either. No doubt they'd gone out to celebrate Manny's appointment to the Ocean Manor Board of Directors.

"What now?" she asked.

"We wait."

She glanced longingly at the door and thought of Nestor's ring of keys. "I don't suppose . . ."

"No, we cannot go in."

She sighed. "I know. It was just wishful thinking."

Just to be sure she didn't get any more dangerous and illegal ideas, Michael guided her to the elevator, his hand firmly in the middle of her back. The power of that totally innocent touch gave her plenty to think about. In the elevator he punched the buttons for her floor and the lobby.

"I've got to get back outside. Go on and get some sleep."

"Brian's out there."

"I'll have Liza bring him in."

Molly was suddenly too exhausted to argue. "You're probably right."

When the doors opened on five, Michael pressed the hold button and gazed down at her. Losing herself in the intensity of that look, Molly almost missed his words.

"In case I've forgotten to mention it, you've been a big help in this," he said.

Still dazed, she murmured, "Me? You think I've helped?"

He grinned at her astonishment.

Molly tucked her hands in her pockets to keep from throwing her arms around his neck. "Well, I'll be damned." That was all she needed to stiffen her resolve. She would discover the killer if she had to stay awake half the night to figure it out.

CHAPTER
SEVENTEEN

Michael hadn't returned by the time Molly left for work in the morning. Apparently, he wasn't having any better luck solving the two crimes than she was. He called, though, at midmorning.

"You okay?" he asked, his voice weary.

"About as tired as you sound," she admitted.

"Didn't you get any sleep?"

"Brian woke up twice with nightmares. I think seeing Ingrid's body made all of this real to him. He was pretty scared. He didn't want me to leave him at school today. It's the first time ever he hasn't been anxious to be rid of me."

"God, I'm sorry. I wish like hell I could wrap this up."

"Any new leads?"

"I've been running a paper chase on Mendoza all day. I want more than suspicions when I finally get to him."

"What have you found?"

"Zip. *Nada*. The guy's so clean, I'm surprised he's not up for sainthood."

"Too clean?"

"Let's just say I always find it a little odd when there's not so much as a traffic ticket on someone's record. Hell, I'd settle for an overtime parking violation. Otherwise I start wondering who's been taking care of them for him."

"The man builds parking lots. Maybe he's never needed to park at a meter."

"I'm too tired for cute, Molly."

"Sorry."

"Watch your step out there today. Don't wander around alone. Okay?"

She didn't need to ask why. She could sense Michael's conviction that the danger had magnified, that for the killer the stakes had gotten bigger than ever. "I'll be careful."

"I'll be by later unless something breaks. Have Liza or someone come by this evening so you and Brian aren't in that apartment alone."

Molly was quiet for several seconds before finally voicing something that had been on her mind. "Maybe I should send Brian to stay with his father for a few days," she said. She had considered that possibility with great reluctance when Brian lay trembling in her arms in the middle of the night. Then she'd thought about the last angry exchange she'd had with Hal DeWitt, the last of many times when he'd suggested she wasn't strong enough to have custody of their son.

"That's up to you," Michael said. "Could be,

though, that he'd be more terrified if he couldn't see
you and know you're okay.''

She thought of Vince's offer to send both of them
to California. If she mentioned it, Michael might very
well insist she take Vince up on it. The truth of the
matter was, though, that she wanted to stay near Michael. Since knowing him and feeling his respect for
her grow, she'd felt herself getting stronger again,
more in charge of her life. Foolhardy or not, she'd
finally realized she really could take care of herself and
Brian. With all that had happened, she hadn't
cracked. She wasn't the inept woman Hal DeWitt had
almost had her believing she was.

''We'll be there, when you get there,'' she said
finally.

''Later, then.''

Later, though, Molly had a brainstorm. It came to
her as she was parking her car that night at the condo.
They had never fully investigated the garage. She and
Michael had both assumed that Allan's fury at Brian
when he caught him playing there was linked to the
fact that the kids were spraying the hose. What if that
weren't the case? What if he'd just made a discovery
and hadn't wanted the kids near it—whatever *it* was—
until he'd had a chance to fully investigate?

With Brian upstairs waiting for her, she didn't
dare take the time to explore now, but she vowed to
get Liza to look after him so she could come back
down. As soon as they'd had dinner, she called Liza.

''Can you come over and stay with Brian for a
while?''

''Sure. What's up? You and the hunk heading out
for the evening?''

"I don't think the *hunk* has time to date in the middle of a murder investigation. If he did, I'm not likely to be the companion of choice."

Liza gave an exaggerated sigh. "Priorities and timing are everything in life, aren't they? So what are you doing?"

"I just have to run an errand."

"Molly DeWitt," Liza said skeptically, "what are you up to?"

"An errand, that's it."

"Exactly what sort of errand are you running that isn't suitable for Brian? Do you have a fetish for X-rated movies you've never mentioned?"

Molly improvised. "He has homework."

"Which he probably finished hours ago."

Exasperated and guilty, Molly retorted, "Are you coming over or not?"

"I'll be right there."

Liza was there in two minutes carrying a baseball bat. Molly's eyes widened. "What on earth is that for?"

"Protection."

"I think you'll be safe enough in here."

"We're not going to be in here. We're coming with you."

"Liza, no. Not a chance."

"I'm not letting you go do whatever you're considering doing on your own. I'll use this on you, if I have to."

She actually sounded as if she meant it. Molly groaned and called Brian. "We're going down to check out the garage to see if we can figure out why Mr. Winecroft got so upset when he found you playing down there."

Brian's eyes grew as wide as Liza's had. "Mom, maybe this isn't such a good idea. Detective O'Hara really won't like it."

"And how do you know so much about what Detective O'Hara likes and doesn't like?"

"He called me this afternoon."

"He did? What did he want?"

"Just to talk and stuff. We made a deal."

"What kind of deal?"

"He said if I'd take care of you, he'd find the killer."

Quite a deal, Molly thought. Apparently, though, it had reassured Brian and that was all that mattered. "You can still keep your bargain. We'll all go to the garage together and we'll tell him everything we find."

Brian frowned. "Jeez, Mom, I don't think that's what he meant."

Molly's expression turned grim. "It's the best deal you're getting from me. We'll be just fine if we stick together. Liza has a bat."

Brian rolled his eyes. "Mom, have you ever seen her play ball? She'd miss an elephant."

Liza looked offended. "See if I ever play with you again, kid."

Molly left the apartment without waiting to see if they followed. She knew there wasn't a chance in hell that they wouldn't.

Ridiculously enough, they found themselves tip-toeing across the concrete in the garage. When they reached the well-lighted greenhouse area, Molly led the way inside. There was nothing spooky or frightening about the escapade so far. Nor was there anything especially revealing. A few pieces of rusted equipment had been abandoned in a plastic tray. Bags of fertilizer and potting soil were stacked in one corner. A hose lay coiled nearby. Other than that, the only things in the greenhouse were growing. A few palms, some more disgustingly healthy impatiens, a scraggly fern in dire need of misting.

Molly kicked at a bag of soil in disgust. "Well, this was certainly a waste of time."

"Maybe not," Liza said slowly.

Molly followed the direction of her gaze. She was staring at one of those portable sheds a few yards away. It was in an assigned parking place. Either an owner had put it there for additional storage or the space had been unsold and the shed belonged to the condominium.

"What's in here?" Liza said moving closer. Molly and Brian were right behind her.

"I'm not sure," Molly said. "I've never even noticed it before. I don't park on this side."

"I've seen it," Brian said. "It's open sometimes in the daytime."

"Have you seen the inside?"

"It's just boxes and stuff."

"Who's had it open?"

"Maintenance guys, people like that."

"Was it open the day you fought with Mr. Winecroft?"

"I don't remember. I don't think so, unless Mr. Winecroft had just closed the door or something. Nobody else was here."

Molly tried the handle. It was locked. "So much for that."

"Wait a second," Liza said. She went back into the

greenhouse and found a piece of wire that had been used to close one of the bags of fertilizer. She twisted it loose and brought it back. An expression of concentration on her face, she jiggled it in the lock for about fifteen seconds and the door swung open.

"How'd you do that?" Brian asked in awe.

"Don't you dare tell him," Molly warned. She scowled at her too curious son. "If I so much as see you within fifty yards of a locked door with a piece of wire in your hands, I'll ground you until you graduate from high school."

"Save the parental lectures," Liza said. "Let's check this out and get out of here."

They stepped inside. The shed was hot and stuffy, its single aisle narrow. Shelves lined both sides. The shelves were crammed with boxes, bottles, and jars of cleaning supplies. Whole drums of liquid carpet shampoo sat on the floor. In all, there was more than it would take to clean Ocean Manor from top to bottom for months on end.

"This hardly seems like the stuff over which murders are committed," Liza said. "I can't tell you the last time I got worked up over copper polish."

"A lot of copper polish," Molly pointed out.

Liza stared at her. "Meaning?"

"Do you know of any copper in our building? Maybe the pipes in the plumbing, but I doubt they spend a lot of time polishing those."

Liza grabbed up a bottle. "Maybe it can be used on brass. See, it says so right here. And there's brass in the elevators."

"Not enough to justify several hundred dollars' worth of polish."

"So maybe the order came in by mistake."

"Then why didn't someone send it back? How much of this was ordered because we need it and how much because somebody got a cut of the action?"

Liza was shaking her head. She gestured around the tiny shed. "The profit on this is peanuts."

"Maybe it's also just the tip of the iceberg. Come on. I want to call Michael and let him know. He can decide if it's important or not. I've got the budget figures upstairs, too. We can see how much all of this cost."

When they got back to the fifth floor, Molly's door was standing wide open. Liza stared down the hall indignantly. "Why, of all the nerve," she said and marched straight toward the apartment, bat upraised.

Molly caught her arm. "Are you out of your mind? Let's go into your place and call the police."

Before they could do that, though, she heard Michael's voice from inside her apartment. He was cussing someone out in a mix of English and Spanish. Molly caught the drift of his displeasure in both languages.

"*Madre de Dios,* are you *loco*? I told you not to let her out of your sight. I don't care if you followed her to the apartment and then sat out front to watch in case she decided to leave again. Didn't it occur to you that she could leave by foot or go someplace else in the building? The killer lives here, dammit!"

Molly touched his shoulder. Michael whirled around, his complexion an exhausted gray under the olive tone. He slammed the phone into the cradle and pulled her into his arms. "Jesus, I thought something had happened to you."

Molly could feel the slam of his heart in his chest, the tension in his muscles as his arms enfolded her. She might very well have stayed right where she was forever, but Michael let her go as a sigh of relief shuddered through him.

"Where have you three been? It took ten years off my life, when I came I here and you were missing. I knocked on every door in the hall. No one had seen you. You promised you'd stay here tonight until I got here."

"We went down to the garage," Molly said meekly, as Liza challenged Brian to a video game and left her alone with Michael.

"Why?"

"It occurred to me we might have missed something the last time."

"Did we?"

"Not in the greenhouse." She told him what they'd found in the storage shed and the significance she'd attributed to it.

"Could be," he admitted. "Where's the budget?"

She found the papers and handed them to him, then waited in silence as he went over the items under supplies. "Hell, I don't know what I'm looking for. I need cleanser, I buy one can of whatever's on sale. I have no idea what constitutes a good deal for a place like this."

"But Manny Mendoza would know."

Michael nodded. "It all keeps coming back to him, doesn't it? I suppose it couldn't hurt to stop by for an unofficial chat."

He was halfway to the door before he realized that Molly was right where he'd left her. He grinned. "You, too. It'll look less official that way. Besides, then I'll know exactly where you are."

CHAPTER
EIGHTEEN

The Mendozas were having a party. At least fifty people were crowded into their penthouse apartment, sipping brandy, following what had apparently been a lavish dinner. The heavy scent of Cuban cigar smoke drifted into the room, even though the smokers had been sent to the balcony for their after-dinner indulgence.

"Molly, how lovely to see you again," Rosa said, looking surprised but delighted. "And Detective O'Hara, isn't it?"

Michael nodded. "Good evening, ma'am. I'm terribly sorry to intrude, but I need to speak with your husband for a moment. Alone, if that's possible."

"Why don't I show you into the den, then?"

As they crossed the living room, Michael greeted several of the Latin men whom Molly recognized as developers and bankers. As soon as Rosa had ushered them into the den and offered them something to drink, she said, "I think Manny's out on the balcony. I'll send him right in."

When Rosa had gone, Molly said, "There were enough power brokers in that room to buy and sell downtown Miami."

"That's probably exactly what they were doing. A lot of deals get made in social settings just like this."

Manny Mendoza came into the room just then, an unlit cigar firmly clamped between his teeth. He took it out and dropped it into an ashtray. "Rosa insisted I give them up. Can't break the habit, though," he muttered. He eyed the offending cigar as if it were responsible for his weakness. Then he smiled. Molly had seen expressions like that before on posters of benign dictators.

"Now, then," he said, taking a seat behind an oversize desk. Under other circumstances the desk's size might be functional. Tonight it was also intimidating, separating him from them, even though his words demonstrated a spirit of cooperation.

"What can I do for you?" he inquired. Shrewd brown eyes seemed to be assessing both Michael and Molly. He dismissed her and concentrated on the detective.

Michael leaned forward. "Mr. Mendoza, I'd like to ask you a few more questions about the night of Allan's murder. I believe you told me you had a meeting that night."

"Yes, a committee of the Latin Developers Association."

"In a Little Havana restaurant, is that right?"

"Versailles, yes."

"Do any of the other men who attended that meeting happen to be here tonight?"

Mendoza's eyes darkened with quick anger, but his voice remained impassive. "Quite a few of them, as a matter of fact."

"I'd appreciate it, if you would point them out to me in a moment."

"Friend," Mendoza began in a decidedly un- friendly tone, then, *"amigo."* With a glance at Molly he launched into a barrage of Spanish. He spoke too rap- idly for her to follow what he was saying, but the in- creasingly furious expression on Michael's face sug- gested that Mendoza had made a very bad miscalculation.

"Mr. Mendoza, that is not how I conduct police business," Michael said. Since his own Spanish was flawless, Molly had the feeling he was deliberately us- ing English as a slap in the man's face. "I don't inten- tionally set out to get Hispanics, nor will I accept a bribe to protect them, and I resent the hell out of the fact that you think I would. Maybe greasing palms is the way you got things done in Cuba. Maybe it still oils wheels for you in Miami. It doesn't cut shit with me."

Mendoza looked offended, though Molly wasn't sure whether it was by the accusation or the obscenity. He held up his hands in a placating gesture. "Detec- tive, please. I meant no offense. I merely asked that you do nothing here tonight. Some critical business matters hang in the balance. I would hate to have them go the wrong way because of your ill-timed ques- tions."

"If world peace hung in the balance, you might not be able to stop me from asking," Michael said, tension radiating from every indignant pore. "I will make every attempt not to upset anyone, but I'm trying to find a killer and some of your guests might be able to help."

"Only if you think that I am the killer, isn't that right? You wish to check my alibi?"

"Exactly."

"And can you not see that someone wishing to do business with me might have grave second thoughts if it were suggested that I might be involved in a murder investigation? Could you not call these people tomorrow? I will give you a list. It would be a favor to me, one I would not forget."

"I told you—"

"I know, and I apologize for any misunderstanding. I see now that you are a man of principle. That does not mean that at some time in the future I would not be able to pay you back for your kindness tonight, perhaps with a word in the right ear."

No matter how Mendoza tried to polish it up, it still sounded like bribery to Molly. She watched Michael's reaction. He continued to look as if he'd tasted water tainted with pond scum.

Sensing that he might be close to victory, despite Michael's expression of distaste, Mendoza said persuasively, "Perhaps you would like to stay, mingle a bit. You could observe, perhaps even ask a discreet question or two. I could trust you to be very discreet, could I not?"

"Fine," Michael said.

"That is wonderful," Mendoza said enthusiastically, beaming at his success. Molly doubted that he experienced losing often. "Come with me. I will have Enrique give you a drink."

At the mention of the guard's name Molly and Michael exchanged glances. Perhaps they would learn more tonight than they'd anticipated only moments earlier.

Michael hesitated at the door to the den. "Where were you last night, Mr. Mendoza?"

"At the condo meeting. You were there, Detective. I'm quite sure you saw me."

"And after the meeting?"

"Rosa and I went to dinner, alone."

"Do you happen to have a credit card slip from the restaurant?"

"I always pay in cash, unless it is for business. However, you could ask. The waiters all know us. They would tell you we were there until nearly midnight. Now, please, follow me."

In the living room, he introduced them to several couples as if they were merely late-arriving guests, then pointed the way to the bar. "Enjoy yourselves. I am delighted you were able to stop by after all."

On their way to the bar, which had been set up near the balcony doors, Molly held Michael back. "Why did you agree to his terms?"

"For one thing, I spotted Enrique as we came in. I wanted a chance to speak with him. For another, it was clear we were getting nowhere with Mendoza. I didn't want his guests getting out of here tonight without my talking with them even if I have to do it discreetly and under Mendoza's watchful eye. You know some of these people, don't you?"

"Some."

"Then you might do a little mingling yourself. See what you can pick up."

"About Mendoza's alibi for the night of Allan's murder?"

"And last night."

Molly nodded. "Anybody in particular you'd like me to approach?"

"Take your pick," he said, handing her a snifter of brandy. He rolled his own expertly around the glass, then took a sip. "God, I hate this stuff. Enrique, I don't suppose you have any beer tucked behind there."

With that he turned his back on Molly and began a friendly conversation with the fired security guard. Left to her own devices, Molly mingled, listening to the flow of conversation around her, much of it in Spanish. Occasionally the sentences would drift from Spanish to English and back again, as if the speaker could express some things more clearly in one language than in another or was, perhaps, unaware of the switches entirely.

It was the head of the Latin Builders Association, a man with whom she'd often dealt when looking for special locations for various producers, who finally approached her. "Molly, you are looking lovely this evening," Xavier Nunez said, brushing his lips across her fingers in an old-world courtly gesture.

Despite the sincerity of the compliment, Molly suddenly realized how inappropriately she was dressed. The other women in the room wore fancy cocktail dresses, dangerously high heels, and enough gold jewelry to pay for a low-budget motion picture. Feeling the need to explain, she gestured at her slacks and blouse and picked up on Mendoza's earlier lead. "I was on a night shoot for a film and was able to get away at the last minute. Manny said to come by no matter how late it was."

"You would be beautiful no matter what you wore, señora. How is the movie business these days?"

"Picking up all the time."

"I have an interesting home you should visit. The architecture is very modern, very Miami. It is almost complete, but the owner will not take possession for a few months yet. I am sure he would be agreeable to having it used in a film. In fact I think he would find it most amusing. I could take you one day next week if you like."

Molly was only half listening by the time he finished. Distracted, she murmured her thanks and moved across the room in the direction in which she'd seen Jack Kingsley go with Manny Mendoza. Why would the manager of the condominium be at a party with the Mendozas and their high-powered friends? She went down the hallway after him, pausing outside the door to the den. It was closed, but she could hear the murmur of voices. If she recalled correctly, there was a bathroom connecting the den and the bedroom next door. Perhaps she could hear more clearly from in there.

Glancing down the hallway, she slipped into the bedroom and peered cautiously through the open doorway to the bath. The door to the den was closed. She went into the bathroom and checked to make sure both doors were locked. Then she listened.

"The board wasn't happy with that last supply,"

Kingsley said. "You'll have to increase the quality this time or I'll have trouble getting an approval."

"You forget that I am back. I will sign off. If I send you a higher grade material, that increases the cost to me. The increase will have to come out of your cut."

"No," Kingsley said. "It comes out of your share. You do what you have to do or I'll find a supplier who can come through for me."

"And who will sign the papers for you?" Mendoza countered. "You lost money those months when Allan was in charge. The college bills for your children did not stop, however, did they? Be sensible, my friend, or one of these days you're going to go too far. In many ways these penny-ante deals of yours are more trouble than they're worth."

Suddenly the picture came clear to Molly. It was the manager, not Mendoza, who'd been behind the purchasing decisions, obviously with Mendoza's cooperation. Mendoza's company was apparently getting its own share of the take.

With his business background and distaste for waste and mismanagement, Allan Winecroft had probably figured out the scam the first time he'd taken a good look at the books. Certainly he would have noticed the first time a major bid came in for supplies and was submitted from Mendoza's firm without competing bids. Even if he hadn't yet figured out who was responsible, if he'd objected strenuously, it would have threatened Kingsley's way of doing business. If he was raking in thousands of dollars a year in kickbacks, that was certainly motive enough for murder. Mendoza had a motive also. Had Allan exposed his role in the scheme, it would have damaged his reputation as a legitimate businessman.

But what about opportunity? Which man had that? And how had either of them known about the matching knives? Was there a set in Kingsley's apartment? Or maybe even in this one? The two of them clearly worked together in everything else. What about the murder? Could they have plotted it together?

Molly slipped out of the bathroom and made her way to the kitchen, where the caterers were just cleaning up. She smiled brightly. "Excuse me, I just wanted to get a plain glass of water. Would you mind?"

One of the women nodded politely, got a glass from the cabinet and filled it with ice and bottled water. Molly sipped it slowly as she glanced around. "This is really quite a kitchen. Mrs. Mendoza has obviously done a lot in here. You must enjoy working for her."

"*Sí,*" the woman said. "She has only the best."

Molly's gaze focused on the butcher block table at the back of the room. A wooden knife holder sat on it. The handles sticking up looked exactly like her own. "Oh, are those those Swiss knives?" she said, already moving toward them. "I've been wanting to buy some, but they're outrageously expensive. Are they good?"

The caterer looked puzzled, but nodded. "*Sí,* very good, very sharp."

Sharp enough to cut through human muscle anyway, Molly thought with a shudder. One by one she lifted them up, glancing at the blades. The paring knife was there, the utility knife, a bread knife, and a meat cleaver. The serrated knife and the carving knife were missing. Either Mendoza was behind the murders after all or Kingsley had had access to his kitchen on occasions other than tonight. Judging from the conversation she'd just heard between the two, it was likely that they met often. In fact, when Mendoza had been president of the board they would have had plenty of opportunities to plan and scheme together without anyone suspecting a thing.

Once he'd been voted off the board and was no longer able to protect Kingsley's unwise decisions, perhaps Mendoza had become a threat, too. She had just heard him suggest that he was about to cut the flow of money into the manager's hands by ending the sweetheart deals he'd been making. By implicating him in the murder of Allan, the manager would have rid himself of all interference so that his shady business could continue as usual. Or Mendoza could have decided to take matters into his own hands.

Her pulse racing with the excitement of her discovery, she went back into the living room and looked for Michael. Though the crowd was much thinner than when they'd arrived, she didn't spot him immediately. She was so busy looking, though, that she didn't see Kingsley coming up beside her. Before she realized he was there, his hand was under her elbow and he was wordlessly guiding her toward the balcony. Uneasy with his peremptory manner and filled with her own suspicions, she balked at the door.

"Please," he said then, smiling. "You look pale. A little air will be good for you. I'm sure you're distraught over seeing Ingrid like that last night."

"I've survived," she said, hanging back. He urged her forward. They were only twelve floors up, but for Molly that was several stories too many. She stayed as far from the metal railing as she could, her back pressed tight against the wall.

"No, my dear, you must see the view," Kingsley said, gesturing widely. "Because it's on a northwest corner, you can see the Coconut Grove skyline across the bay. It really is lovely from here, especially at night."

At Molly's failure to respond, a flicker of shrewd awareness sparked in his eyes. "Oh, that's right," he said with exaggerated innocence. "Heights make you nervous, don't they?"

Molly was trying to keep her teeth from chattering. She stared at the floor. Every time she dared a glance at Kingsley himself, she glimpsed beyond him and automatically calculated the drop to the ground. Dizziness swept over her.

"How do you know that?" she asked, her voice choked.

"I believe you mentioned it when you moved in. You said you could never live on a floor higher than the fire ladders could reach. That's why you picked the apartment on five, even though we had one available with a nicer view and a better deal."

Terrific, the sadist knew all about her fear of heights and had brought her out here anyway. She had to keep him talking. Sooner or later Michael would miss her and come looking. If she stayed calm and didn't look down, she'd be just fine. Maybe if she acted nonchalant, he would let her go, satisfied with having frightened her.

"Was there something you wanted to talk to me about?" she asked in the closest thing she could manage to a conversational tone. "If not, I'd like to go back inside. Detective O'Hara will be looking for me."

She took a step toward the door, but Kingsley's hand clamped around her elbow so tightly that she knew there'd be bruises by morning. He yanked her closer to the edge. Even though the railing was waist high and reasonably sturdy, Molly could feel bile rising in her throat. She tried to tell herself to remain calm, to keep talking, maybe get him to confirm some of her suppositions about what had happened. But that would mean telling him that she knew the truth and something warned her that would be the most dangerous thing she could do.

Or would it? Even if he was guilty, maybe she could bargain with him. Was it possible to bargain with a man who'd killed twice? Wasn't that what Ingrid had tried? Her attempt at blackmail had certainly backfired.

"You won't do it," she said with far more bravado than she was feeling.

His smile sent chills down her spine. "Do what? I am merely showing you the view." He backed away a step. "I am sorry if you were frightened."

He sounded very sincere. "Perhaps I should get you a drink. Wine? Brandy?"

The manager appeared so concerned Molly was caught off guard. She wondered if she'd been imagining the menace only seconds before. "No, thanks," she said hurriedly. "I was just getting ready to leave."

He nodded and stepped aside. "A pleasure seeing you as always."

Molly shivered. She had to force herself not to

turn and run. Inside she spotted Michael, moved toward him and linked her arm through his. Though he kept talking, there was a quizzical expression in his eyes when he glanced at her. As soon as there was a lull in the conversation, she said, "I really want to get back to Brian. Are you about ready to leave?"

"Not quite yet," he said.

"Then I'll see you downstairs."

He regarded her worriedly. "Molly?"

"It's okay," she told him. "Really." Still shaken, she practically raced from the room. As soon as the door to the Mendoza apartment closed behind her, Molly released the breath she'd been holding. She was in such a hurry to get back to the relative sanctity of her own apartment, she almost took the stairs, then thought of being trapped in the stairwell with Kingsley or Mendoza after her. Again, a chill raced down her spine. She punched the button for the elevator again and again.

"Dammit, come on," she muttered, already regretting the impulse that had made her flee Michael's side. Too late now. She'd be fine, though, once she was home.

The elevator doors slid open and she stepped inside. They had begun to close all too slowly, when hands braced the two sides apart. The doors retracted and Kingsley stepped in. "If you don't mind," he said. "I'll just ride along with you."

Instinctively, Molly reached for the emergency button to set off an alarm, but the manager was quicker. Stepping neatly between her and the control panel, he pressed the button for the garage.

With every ounce of bravado she possessed, Molly said, "Hit five for me, please."

There was that slick, fake smile again as he said, "Not quite yet. There's something I'd like you to see first."

"What?"

"Don't be so impatient. We'll be there in just a minute."

In the garage he grabbed her elbow as roughly as he had earlier and guided her toward the greenhouse and toolshed. When they reached the shed, he opened the lock and shoved her inside. Molly knew she had to keep him talking, had to keep him from locking that door and leaving her in this metal box to die of the heat, if she didn't die of sheer terror first.

"Why are you doing this?" she demanded, hoping for a confession she could pass along when she got out of this.

"Don't play games with me. I know you've figured everything out. I saw you try to slip away from the bathroom after my meeting with Mendoza upstairs. You went straight to the kitchen to check on the knives, didn't you?"

There was little point in denying it, she decided. "Did Mendoza kill Allan?" she asked, hoping that casting blame elsewhere would buy her a little time. Instead, Jack Kingsley looked insulted.

"Please," he said derisively.

Molly was startled by the too easy admission. Then, again, what could it matter? He was going to leave her here to die. Obviously he saw no reason not to tie up any loose ends for her satisfaction before he shut her in and locked the door.

"Okay, how did you know about the knives? It was very clever of you."

"Drucilla sliced a piece of cake for me when I dropped by the cardroom later that night. I didn't realize the knife was yours at the time, but the opportunity was too good to miss. When she'd taken it with her, I slipped upstairs, used the master key, and borrowed one from the Mendozas' kitchen. I figured I had two people in line in front of me as suspects. The owner of the first knife and Mendoza. Should have been the perfect crime. It would have been, too, if it hadn't been for that foolish girl. Ingrid had borrowed one of Rosa's knives one night and recognized that it and the murder weapon came from the same set. She had seen me coming from the Mendozas' apartment the night of the murder and put two and two together. She tried to blackmail me. I couldn't let her get away with it."

"So you killed her last night."

"I had no choice, just as I have none now."

Molly guessed his next move and tried to grab him as he backed out of the shed. She caught the edge of his sleeve and heard it rip as he shook her off, then slammed the door with a metallic crash. She threw herself against it, but it didn't give. She picked herself up and prepared to make one last desperate attempt, but she heard the ominous click as the door locked.

"Oh God," she muttered, sliding to the floor. "Oh, damn."

CHAPTER
NINETEEN

Twice during the endless, sweltering night Molly heard the distant sound of car doors closing. Each time she pounded on the walls of the shed and screamed at the top of her lungs. Each time she failed to attract any attention.

Morning would be better, she told herself repeatedly. More people would be coming and going. Perhaps someone from maintenance would even come to open the shed for supplies. Surely by then Michael would have launched a full-scale search as well. It would be okay.

But all the time she sought to reassure herself, she could feel the perspiration trickling down her back, feel the heat closing in and the air getting more and more stale and lifeless.

Inch by inch she searched the shed for some sort of tool that could be used as a lever on the door. Surely it couldn't take too much strength to pop the hinges on a temporary structure like this. The only thing she found was a supply of mop handles, and those couldn't be wedged into the tiny slit between the door and its frame.

She finally sank onto one of the boxes and tried to think. She needed to conserve her strength, too. Perspiring too freely would only speed the heat prostration she was facing if she wasn't found soon. It was too dark inside to see her watch, but from the way the heat was building, she could tell it was daylight. As the sun rose, so would the temperature in the shed. She had no idea how long a person could survive in that sort of intense heat, but it probably wasn't long. Hours, perhaps.

Bordering on panic, she began taking shallower and shallower breaths as perspiration dried and her skin burned feverishly. For something to do, she began counting supplies. Fifty ten-gallon drums of rug shampoo. Ten, no, twelve boxes of extra-large-size bottles of liquid soap. Five, no, eight—oh, God, how many cartons of paper towel rolls? They seemed to be swimming in front of her eyes. She licked her lips, surprised to find them already dry and cracked.

From what seemed to be very far away she heard voices. She had to signal them, had to make them hear her. She tried to scream, but her throat was dry, so very dry. With the last of her strength, she heaved a can of copper polish at the metal wall. It clattered noisily to the floor. She repeated the gesture again and again, for once grateful to Kingsley for the absurdly large order.

"Over here," someone shouted from nearby.

She heard footsteps, then Michael. *"Madre de*

Dios," he said, swearing impatiently. "Get it open. Molly, it's okay. We'll have you out in just a minute."

She could hear more curses, the jangle of keys, then finally the lock being tried. She struggled to her feet, but immediately sagged back down. The door was flung wide and Michael caught her just before she hit the floor.

She looked into his worried eyes and murmured, "What the hell took you so long?" And then she fainted.

When she came to, she was in a hospital bed, hooked up to an IV, a strange doctor hovering over her and Michael lurking watchfully in the background.

"It was Kingsley," she whispered, even though it hurt her parched throat to speak.

"I know. We got him. Mendoza finally confessed everything about the kickback scheme. While he was spilling his guts last night, one of the caterers came out and told him two of his knives were missing. I guess they didn't want to be blamed. They said you'd been snooping around in the kitchen. We looked for you, but both you and Kingsley had left the party. I swear to God the last eighteen hours have taken a dozen years off my life thinking he had you. We couldn't find Kingsley, even though we put out an all points bulletin. The Miami Beach police thought they spotted his car over there. Then we got a call from Bal Harbor. The Hollywood cops finally stopped him about forty minutes ago. When I realized you weren't with him, I nearly lost it. We tore the condo apart looking for you. It was Liza who suggested the shed because of what you all had found there earlier."

Because she couldn't deal with the emotions she thought she saw in his eyes, she said, "Brian?"

"He's right outside. I'll get him."

Barely a minute later, her son burst through the door and threw himself into her arms. His thin chest was heaving with sobs. Michael laid a hand on Brian's head, gently smoothing the light-brown hair that was damp with perspiration and tears.

Michael's gaze, though, was on Molly. "I have things I have to take care of at headquarters," he said quietly. "And you and Brian need some time alone."

Molly bit back her own cry of need and nodded.

He hesitated, his expression uncertain. "I could hang around if you need me."

She shook her head, not trusting herself to speak, not trusting herself not to beg him to stay now that his official duties were over.

"I'll be back when we have this all sorted out, okay?" The sunglasses went on then, but not before she caught the vulnerability that was all too evident in his eyes. He turned away.

Michael had taken several slow steps, when Molly called to him. "You are coming back?"

He nodded. "As soon as I can get here."

After he'd gone Liza took up his place beside Molly's bed. With Brian in her arms she fell asleep. When she awoke, Liza was still there and Brian was still sound asleep and clinging to Molly's hand.

For the first time since Molly had known her, Liza looked as if she were at a loss for words. "You want something to drink?" she asked finally.

"No, but you look as if you could use something." Molly touched her shoulder. "Are you okay?"

Liza finally met her gaze, tears streaking down her face. "It's funny. You two are the closest thing to family I have. When we realized you were missing, I wanted to trade places with you. I was so terrified of what would happen." Her voice trailed off and she glanced at Brian.

Molly shuddered and stroked his hair. "I know. Me, too. It's the only thing that kept me going," she whispered, looking down at her son.

They sat quietly for several minutes before Liza murmured, "You're falling in love with the hunk, aren't you?"

Molly managed a grim smile. "If I had to put a label on what I'm feeling, I'd say I'm falling in love with the *possibility* of falling in love again. Michael possesses certain traits, a certain strength and sensitivity, that would make it easy to love him. He also has a few that drive me nuts."

"The man is hot, Molly. Why don't you sleep with him? That ought to clarify things."

"Or confuse them more than ever."

"How does he feel?"

"I don't know. Bianca's still in his life. I can't deny her existence. I can't wish her away."

"What does he say?"

"Not much, at least not on that subject."

The knock on the door startled them both. Liza grinned. "I think that's your answer now."

"Has it been that long?"

"I suspect he was in a hurry. I'll let him in and let myself out. Is there anything you need from home?"

Molly ran shaky fingers through her hair trying to sort out the tangles. She suddenly regretted not being able to take a shower, change into something besides this frumpy hospital gown, and put on makeup. How had she let the time slip away when she'd known Michael was coming back? Maybe she'd just been telling herself that this meeting wasn't significant, even though the thumping of her heart right now felt like a drum in a Sousa march.

"You look good," Michael said from across the room, when Liza had gone taking the still sleepy Brian with her.

A near-hysterical giggle climbed in Molly's throat, but she managed to swallow it.

"Your color's better."

"It usually is, when every drop of blood hasn't drained out of my face," she said wryly. "I've never been so terrified in my life."

He rocked back on his heels, hands in his pockets as if he wasn't sure what else to do with them. "Me, too."

"Because I was an innocent bystander who almost got killed? Afraid you'd slipped up in your duty, Detective?"

His lips twitched at her deliberate ploy. "No, Mrs. DeWitt, because you're you and for better or worse you've gotten under my skin."

"Sounds like an allergy."

He dared a step closer, looked around, and chose a chair about as far from her as he could get and still be in the same room. Molly shook her head, very much aware of his confusion. "You don't have to stay. I'm fine and you wouldn't be responsible even if I weren't."

"I feel responsible and . . ."

When he didn't go on, she prodded, "And?"

He shook his head. "I don't know what the hell to do about this. First of all, there's . . ."

Molly ignored the sting of tears and snapped, "Bianca. For crying out loud, you can say her name. I'm not that fragile."

He nodded slowly, his eyes troubled. "Yes, there is Bianca. On top of that, I'm not such a good bet when it comes to anything serious. I learned that being married. Being a cop and marriage just don't mix."

"You've taken an amazing leap of faith here. I thought we were talking about maybe having a date. You're worried about what happens after the wedding."

"Dates have a way of leading to marriage before you know what's happened."

"Not when you have two rational, thoughtful, very cautious people involved."

That drew a genuine smile that put sparks into his brown eyes. "Cautious, huh? You, too?"

"Damn right. I'm in no rush for any kind of commitment."

He nodded again. "So, you're willing to risk a date or two?"

"If anything happens to change your living arrangements, yes. But that's your decision, Detective. I'm not asking you to and I'm not making any promises after that."

"Fair enough." He stood up then and started toward the door. "I'll be in touch."

Molly clutched the flat hospital pillow so hard all

the stuffing was squashed into one end. She managed a wobbly smile. "You do that."

"You'll be okay tonight?"

"Fine." *Just go! Go before I make an absolute fool of myself,* she thought desperately.

Before she realized what he intended, though, he was across the room, apparently propelled by the same barrage of contradictory feelings that had her off-balance. He cupped her chin and tilted her head until their gazes clashed. He leaned down then until his lips brushed tenderly across hers. That faint, tentative whisper of a touch was filled with so much longing, so much purely sensual promise, that it left Molly weak.

"See you," he said.

"Yeah. See you." Her tone was so determinedly casual she could have been saying good-bye to the exterminator.

He was shaking his head. "No, no, sweetheart. When I say I'll see you, I mean it."

"Of course you will," she said jauntily. "If you're going to let Brian play soccer on your team, we're bound to run into each other."

"You talk way too much," he said, his mouth covering hers again. This time there was nothing sweet and tender about the kiss. This time the sensation was far more primal, filled with wicked heat and dangerous passion.

This time, when Michael walked away, Molly knew he'd be back. She believed in that much, at least.

April 1992

Dear Readers:

It's probably very important to note that while I do live in a condominium on Key Biscayne, it is not the fictitious Ocean Manor of this book. Without making it clear that this work is entirely a product of my imagination, I might well be run off my island paradise. Likewise the characters of the Miami/Dade Film Commission are pure inventions, though I am grateful to former director Dick Renick and his staff for their insights into filmmaking in Miami.

In future Molly DeWitt Romantic Mysteries, I plan to share more of this fascinating, diverse, and dynamic South Florida locale with you. I hope you'll join Molly, Brian, Liza, and the very sexy Detective O'Hara for future *hot* Miami adventures.

Your comments, as always, would be greatly appreciated. Send a self-addressed, stamped envelope for a response to P.O. Box 490326, Key Biscayne, FL 33149.

Wishing you a life filled with mystery and romance.

Sherryl Woods

Be sure to catch Sherryl Woods's
next exciting romantic mystery,

HOT SECRET

coming soon from Dell.

CHAPTER
ONE

Anyone who considered filmmaking glamorous had never been on a movie set at the end of a twelve-hour day. And at ten P.M. on a Saturday night, tempers tended to be frayed beyond repair. Veronica Weston's dressing room trailer, half a block long and complete with kitchen, practically reverberated with the echoes of an argument that had begun at dawn and gotten noisier and nastier with each passing hour. If anyone knew the gist of the star's complaint, it wasn't being shared with Molly DeWitt, who'd been assigned by the Miami/Dade Film Commission to keep everyone happy. Judging from the shouts, she wasn't doing a wonderful job.

Hot, tired, and drained from the nonstop tension, Molly sat at the Cardozas' porch-front café in Miami Beach's rejuvenated Art Deco district and sipped her tenth iced tea since dinnertime. If she hadn't been working, she would have ordered something a lot more lethal. The thought of a piña colada or a strawberry daiquiri held an almost irresistible appeal.

The door of Veronica's trailer crashed open and the star emerged in a dramatic swirl of hot-pink chiffon that was more suited to a boudoir than to a public place. She caught sight of Molly and made a beeline for her table. She flounced into a chair amid a cloud of pink. It was indicative of the neighborhood, a haven for trendy yuppies and high-fashion European models, that no one paid the slightest attention.

"That man," she said in reference to the film's director, Gregory Kinsey, "has the talent of a toad. I will not listen to another word he says."

Since Veronica was making her comeback film after years of alcoholic decline, Molly thought it prudent to suggest a spirit of improved cooperation. "I'm sure he has your best interests at heart," she suggested.

"Ha!" Veronica gestured to a passing waiter and ordered a double vodka on the rocks. She didn't seem worried about either slipping off the wagon or falling down drunk in her final shot of the night.

"After all, it is his reputation on the line as well," Molly ventured, feeling infinitely braver since her first observation hadn't drawn fire. She didn't dare suggest that Gregory Kinsey, whose last two pictures had been Academy Award nominees, hadn't needed to take a risk on a woman who'd dragged her own last two films into over-budget box office debacles. Besides, she felt a certain amount of sympathy for the fifty-something actress, whose once gorgeous face and career had been ravaged by alcohol. She admired the spunk it had taken to ignore all of the vicious tabloid gossip and return to the screen in a less than flattering role, a role Kinsey reportedly had fought to offer her. The fact that the two had been at loggerheads since the first day of production was no secret, and Molly wondered why the up-and-coming Gregory had bothered trying to salvage the woman's down-sliding career.

Veronica gulped down the drink and ordered another. "You know, dear, you're really wasting your time in this town," she said, giving Molly a critical once-over. "You ought to move to LA. That's where the industry is. Half the producers in that town would kill to have someone who could keep things organized the way you do. Does that boss of yours, Vince what's-his-name, appreciate you?"

The concept of Vince displaying gratitude was enough to make Molly smile. "No, but I happen to love Miami," she said. "And I'm not the issue, you are. What will it take to make you happy? Is there something I can do to make this shoot easier on you?"

Veronica seemed startled that anyone honestly cared what she wanted now that her stardom had crashed. "Maybe you could go talk to Gregory," she said, slowly warming to the idea. "He'd listen to you.

He's surrounded by all those sycophants. I haven't seen so much bowing and scraping since I met the queen. Did I ever tell you that story, dear? Well, never mind, now's not the time. You go speak to Gregory and then we'll talk about all that ancient history."

Molly was flattered by Veronica's faith in her persuasiveness, but she seriously doubted that the director was the least bit interested in her amateur opinions. From what she'd observed this past week on the set, Gregory Kinsey had a pretty good idea of exactly what he wanted in every shot. Barely into his thirties and riding an artistic high, he wasn't the type of director to encourage input. "What exactly is the problem between you two?" she asked.

"This god-awful script is the problem. Have you read it? Does it make a bit of sense to you? No," she answered before Molly could comment. "Of course not. No woman my age is going to chase around after some worthless twerp like Rod Lukens. What kind of name is that anyway? He sounds like some cowboy drifter."

Since the entire plot of *Endless Tomorrows* was created around just such a chase, Molly couldn't help inquiring, "Why did you take the role, if you hate it so much?"

Veronica directed one of her famous disbelieving glances at Molly. The subtle lift of one delicate brow spoke volumes on-screen and off. "Offers have not exactly been rolling in the last few years. Everybody wants young. Everybody wants sexy. They seem to forget there's an audience out there that's my age, that women my age can be sexy. I decided I owed it to my gender to prove that."

"And you needed the work."

Veronica laughed, a bawdy, raucous sound that carried on the ocean breeze. "Hell, yes, I needed the work. Do you have any idea how much a stay at that detox clinic costs?"

"Then I'm surprised you're so anxious to repeat it," Molly said with a pointed look at the second double vodka sitting in front of the actress.

Veronica didn't seem to take offense. "Don't worry about me, honey. I'm just getting my second wind. When Gregory calls for action, I'll be in front of the camera, hitting my mark and delivering my lines, no matter how absurd they are. The bottom line is I'm a professional and Gregory knows it. He's counting on it, in fact. He'll let me rant and rave all I want as long as I show up."

"So the tantrum's just for show?"

"Essentially," Veronica admitted with a shrug. "Maybe he'll make a few little changes to pacify me, but he knows I can't afford to walk away from this project, no matter what I say."

"Then why bother? Doesn't all this tension upset you? How can you possibly be creative in the midst of all this angst? I can't finish a grocery list if I'm under a lot of stress."

Veronica threw back her head, setting a shoulder-length wave of chestnut hair into sensuous motion. "Tension, honey? You call this tension? This is just a warm-up. You wait until we get to the love scene and I refuse to get into bed with that sleazy character until he washes that gunk out of his greasy hair.''

Molly had to admit that Duke Lane's insistence on wearing a slicked-back hair style for the role of Miami Beach gigolo Rod Lukens was enough to make her own stomach churn. It might, however, be difficult to get him to step out of character in mid-production and wash his hair. "How do you plan on winning that one?'' she asked.

"I've been thinking about a sexy shower scene which includes a bottle of shampoo. What do you think?'' There was an impish gleam in Veronica's vivid green eyes as she contemplated the prospect.

Molly grinned back at her. "A stroke of genius.''

"Yeah. Now if I could just figure out how to get him to try the mouthwash, too,'' she said wearily. She finished her drink and glanced at her watch. "What the hell is slowing things down now? God, I hate night shoots. They drag on forever. If the cameras don't roll soon, I'm going to have bags under my eyes the size of airline carryons. Honey, could you go check for me? If we're not starting soon, I'm going back inside to rest.''

"No problem,'' Molly said. "I'll be right back. Any idea where Gregory is?''

"Probably in the production trailer trying to figure out how he got himself mixed up in this dud.''

Molly cut through the Saturday night crowd milling along Ocean Drive past the string of hotels that had been painted the colors of dawn on the Atlantic —palest pink, mauve, turquoise, and sun-bleached white. Front porches that had once seen no more action than the squeaking of a rocking chair now served as swank outdoor cafés. Swimming pools had become the focal point of trendy sidewalk bars. On Thirteenth Street, which had been blocked off to accommodate the production, she passed Veronica's trailer and went on to the slightly smaller RV parked in front. A plastic sign declaring GK PRODUCTIONS, END-LESS TOMORROWS was plastered on the side.

Molly tapped on the trailer door and opened it. A handful of exhausted-looking, jeans-clad men were collapsed into the chairs around a rectangular table along one side of the long, narrow room. One of them was playing solitaire while the others sipped sodas and watched in apparent boredom.

"Anybody in here seen Gregory?" she asked, stepping inside long enough to savor the Arctic temperature.

"He's with Veronica."

"No. She's been outside at one of the cafés with me for the past twenty minutes."

The legs of one tilted-back chair hit the floor with a thud. "Shit, man, not again," assistant director Hank Murdock muttered as he lumbered to his feet. "Come on, guys. Let's go find him."

"Find him?" Molly repeated. "You think he's taken off or something?"

"The street is crawling with broads and bars and bedrooms. Greg's not known for overlooking any of those opportunities, especially when they come in combination," Hank said in weary resignation.

"Does that mean you're going to have to shut down production for the night? Should I tell Veronica she can go back to her hotel?"

"Not yet. Tell her to hang loose. We may get this last shot in yet. Jerry, you check Veronica's trailer just to be sure he's not still in there. That's the last place any of us saw him. Maybe he stuck around to recuperate once Veronica got her claws out of him."

"Don't panic, man," Jerry said. "It could be he's with Daniel setting up the next shot."

"I'll check, but I'm not holding my breath."

Molly walked with Jerry as far as the star's trailer. "You all don't like Veronica much, do you?" she said to the young production assistant. He was only twenty-three, but this was his third film with Gregory Kinsey.

"She's making Greg crazy. That's not good for him, and it's not good for the film. Other than that, I don't much think about her one way or the other." For his age he managed an incredible air of bored cynicism.

"Why do you suppose she gets to him? Surely he's worked with other difficult actresses."

"Beats me. I'd have told her to take a hike the first day, but Greg wouldn't budge. He wanted her on this picture no matter what. Fought the studio and everyone else till he got his way." Jerry rapped on the trailer door and waited. When no one answered, he peered inside. "Oh, hell," he muttered, the color draining out of his face. He leaned against the side of the trailer and drew in a couple of deep breaths before shouting at the top of his lungs, "Hank, guys, get the hell over here."

"What is it?" Molly said, trying to peer past him. Jerry blocked her way. He wasn't quite big enough, though, to keep her from spotting one dungaree-clad leg and a trickle of blood running along beside it. She recognized Gregory Kinsey's well-worn cow-boy boot. She swallowed hard and forced her eyes away. "Shouldn't you get inside and do something?"

"Sweetheart, there's not much you can do for a guy who's got a hole the size of a quarter straight through his head."

From the bestselling author of
The Naked Heart

JACQUELINE BRISKIN

☐ **The Naked Heart**
A passionate and unforgettable story of a love that bridges
continents, vengeance that spans generations and a friendship
that triumphs over tragedy.

20563-8 $5.95

☐ **The Onyx**
The sweeping, spectacular story of America's first billionaire, the
woman he loved but could not marry, and the son who threat-
ened to destroy it all.
"Has the feel of a winner."—*Publishers Weekly*
"A compelling yarn."—*Los Angeles Times*

16667-5 $5.95

☐ **Rich Friends**
Em, Caroline, and Beverly came of age in the blue sky days of
postwar California. Now it's their children's turn. But times
have changed and not even their rich friends can save them from
the tragedy that will ultimately touch them all.
"Evocative and moving."—*Publishers Weekly*
"Good storytelling, suspense and a wow ending."
— *San Francisco Chronicle*   17380-9 $4.95